Betty Crocker's

BOYS
AND
GIRLS
MICROWAVE
COOKBOOK

MELISSA HARDTKE

MIKE DECHAINE

CARRIE GRENZ

ALISHA KITCHEN

Betty Crocker's

BOYS
AND
GIRLS
MICROWAVE
COOKBOOK

PRENTICE HALL

New York ● London ● Toronto

Sydney ● Tokyo ● Singapore

PRENTICE HALL GENERAL REFERENCE
15 Columbus Circle
New York, New York 10023

Library of Congress Cataloging-in-Publication Data

Crocker, Betty.
   [Boys and girls microwave cookbook]
   Betty Crocker's boys and girls microwave cookbook.
     p.   cm.
   Includes index.
   Summary: A collection of 100 microwave recipes for snacks, dinners, desserts, and other meals.
   ISBN 0-13-085549-9
   1. Microwave cookery—Juvenile literature. [1. Microwave cookery. 2. Cookery.] I. Title.
TX832.C74 1992
  641.5'882—dc20   91-36493
                             CIP
                             AC

Designed by Levavi & Levavi
Manufactured in the United States of America

10 9 8 7 6 5 4 3 2 1

First Edition

GENERAL MILLS, INC.
Editor: Jean E. Kozar
Test Kitchen Home Economist: Mary H. Johnson
Recipe Copy Editor: Deb Hance
Editorial Assistant: Elaine Mitchell
Food Stylists: Cindy Lund, Mary Sethre
Photographer: Nanci Doonan Dixon
Photography Assistant: Scott Wyberg
Director, Betty Crocker Food and Publications Center: Marcia Copeland
Assistant Manager, Publications: Lois Tlusty

PRENTICE HALL
Publisher: Nina D. Hoffman
Vice President and Editor-in-Chief: Gerard Helferich
Executive Editor: Rebecca W. Atwater
Editor: Anne Ficklen
Assistant Editor: Rachel Simon
Photographic Director: Carmen Bonilla
Illustrator: Laurie Lee Davis
Production Manager: Lessley Davis
Production Editors: Vincent J. Janoski and Kimberly Ann Ebert

CONTENTS

INTRODUCTION

Welcome to the terrific world of microwave cooking! We know how much of a help you can be in the kitchen, so we decided to write a microwave cookbook just for kids. All of these recipes are delicious and many, such as Robot Snacks and Launching Rocket Cones, are especially fun to make.

You can be sure that all of these recipes are great-tasting, because they've all been tested by kids. Boys and girls between the ages of 8 and 12 prepared these recipes in their own homes. You will "meet" many of these hometesters through their pictures and comments accompanying lots of the recipes. The kids had fun testing the recipes and were eager to share their thoughts with you. They suggested ways to improve the recipes and even gave terrific names to some of them. Our hometesters helped us make the best possible cookbook for you.

Many of you use the microwave to prepare after-school snacks or make quick hot breakfasts. If you lend a hand with dinner or lunch, you know that sometimes it's hard to think of new recipes to prepare. In this book you'll find such super recipes as Terrific Tacos, Shoestring and Cheese Pie and Pineapple Puddle Cakes that you'll love to try.

While you'll be able to make many of these recipes by yourself, it's always best to check with an adult before you start. There are important things you should know about safety before you use anything in the kitchen, including the microwave. Look for the special stoplight with every recipe that tells you if help from an adult is needed. Be sure to read the explanation of the stoplight system on the next page.

Microwave cooking is often called "cool cooking" because the kitchen and the microwave don't get hot. The food and the dishes can get hot, however, so make sure to use potholders when handling hot dishes. Please follow recipe instructions carefully; we want your cooking to be fun, delicious and safe! Be sure to clean up after yourself when you use the kitchen—your family will really appreciate it.

We've had a great time creating these special recipes and working with our kid testers. We're sure you too will have lots of fun making the recipes for yourself, your family and your friends.

THE BETTY CROCKER EDITORS

INTRODUCTION TO MICROWAVE MAGIC

Safety Signals

Look for the safety signal traffic light next to each recipe. It will tell you what kind of help you need to make the recipe.

 Red Light: These recipes definitely must be done with adult help. Be sure to have potholders on hand. In these recipes, the food will get hot, a sharp knife may be used for cutting, and there may be hot liquid to handle or hot food for an adult to drain.

 Yellow Light: Recipes where the microwave cooking time is longer and dishes may get warm. Always use potholders, and be sure an adult is available to help.

 Green Light: Recipes that are easy to prepare and only warm in the microwave. The dishes usually do not heat up because the food is being warmed and the dish has handles. It's nice to have an adult available to answer any questions.

For the Cook

You and your friends may call microwave cooking by many names, such as "mike-ing," "waving" or even "nuking." We like to call it microwaving! Whatever you call it, there are some special things to learn and remember as you begin cooking with the microwave:

- Learn how to set the controls on the microwave correctly. Ask an adult to show you how.

- Be sure you can easily reach and see into the microwave. If it's not easy for you to reach, ask an adult to help you with your recipes. It's important to be able to see inside your microwave to follow cooking directions in the recipes.

- Recipes in this cookbook were tested using microwaves with 600 to 650 watts. You're probably used to high, medium and low speeds when riding your bike. Microwaves also have "speeds" called "watts." They are sold from 400 to 800 watts, and we've used the medium, 600–650 watt, cooking speed.

- Ask an adult what the wattage of *your* microwave is. If it's lower than what we tested (say, 500 watts), you may have to add cooking time. If it's higher than we tested (say, 750 watts), check foods at the minimum cooking time or even 30 seconds less than the shortest time given in the recipe.

- Always have potholders on hand and ready to use when handling hot dishes.

- Be careful when touching the dishes in which foods were microwaved. While the dish might not be hot right away, heat can quickly move from the hot food to the dish and make it hot.

- Be very careful when taking your first bite of microwaved food. Moist foods (like the jelly in a sweet roll) get hot much quicker than drier foods (like a plain doughnut).

For the Cook's Helper

Children love to cook and the microwave is one of the safest cooking appliances in the kitchen! But there are some precautions that you should keep in mind. Microwave cooking always results in a change of food temperature, for example, when food is defrosted, or more frequently, when food is heated. Children need to be taught the differences between microwave and conventional cooking.

Your supervision along with some simple rules can make it fun, and more importantly, safe for boys and girls to fix their own snacks and help prepare meals. You are the best judge of the age at which children should be allowed to use the microwave, other kitchen appliances and sharp knives. They need to understand that even though the microwave doesn't get hot, the food does. Follow these simple steps to help children microwave safely:

- We recommend adult supervision whenever children use the microwave. See the Safety Signals, page 1.

- The microwave the children use should be located where it is easy for them to reach the controls as well as put foods in and take foods out safely, without the risk of spilling.

- Children should be taught how to set the controls correctly and use the microwave safely. Please read your microwave's use and care book and teach children any special "do's and don'ts" noted by the microwave manufacturer.

- Microwave dishes used by children should have easy-to-grasp handles and be lightweight for easiest handling. Children cannot tolerate as much heat as adults, and it's normal for heat from microwaved food to transfer to the dish itself, possibly causing accidents or even burns.

- Provide potholders in a size that's easy for smaller, less adept hands to use.

- Teach children safe food-preparation techniques and how to handle hot foods.

Let's Get Started!

Before You Start

- Check with an adult to make sure it's a good time to use the kitchen.

- If you have long hair, tie it back so it won't get in your way.

- Wash your hands and put on an apron.

- Read the recipe all the way through before starting to cook. Ask an adult to explain anything you don't understand.

- Gather all of the ingredients and utensils for the recipe before you start. That way, you'll be sure to have everything you need. Measure all the ingredients carefully. Put everything the recipe lists on a tray. When the tray is empty, you'll know you haven't left anything out!

- Reread the recipe to make sure you haven't left anything out.

While You Cook

- Clean up as you cook—it means less work at the end! When you finish with a utensil (except for sharp knives), put it in warm soapy water to soak. Wash sharp knives separately, and be careful of the blades.

Finishing Up

- Wash and dry all the utensils you have used, and put them away. Wash the counters, and leave the kitchen neat and clean.

- Wash out the microwave with soap and water if anything spilled. If the top of the stove was used, check to be sure the controls are turned off and that the stove top is clean.

- Leaving the kitchen clean will make everyone glad to have you cook again.

Playing It Safe in the Kitchen

PREPARING THE FOOD

- Before you use the microwave or a sharp knife, be sure an adult is in the kitchen to help you and to answer any questions.

- Always dry your hands after you wash them so you won't have slippery fingers.

- Wipe up any spills right away to avoid slipping on the floor.

- When slicing or chopping ingredients, be sure to use a cutting board.

- Always turn the sharp edge of a knife or vegetable peeler away from you and your hand when you chop or peel foods.

- Always use potholders when handling hot dishes to avoid burns.

WHEN YOU'RE COOKING

- Watch for the special directions in each recipe that warn you about hot utensils and foods.

- Carefully uncover casseroles by lifting the lid away from you to let the steam out. Keep your face away from the steam. Remove waxed paper coverings by lifting the corner farthest from you to let the steam out before removing the waxed paper completely.

- If you use the top of the stove, ask an adult for help. Put large pans on large burners, small pans on small burners. Turn the handles of pans so they don't stick out over the edge of the stove where they might get bumped accidentally. Make sure handles don't hang over another burner.

- Ask an adult to drain foods cooked in lots of hot water (like spaghetti). Pans full of hot water are heavy, and if the water isn't poured off just right, the liquid and steam could burn you.

- Be careful where you put hot dishes. Put them on dry surfaces only, ones that won't be hurt by heat.

Microwave Safety Tips

As with other appliances in the home, the microwave should always be used properly. Here are some good rules to follow:

- Read and follow all directions in the manufacturer's use-and-care manual.

- Food can heat unevenly—it can be much hotter at the outside edges than in the middle or at the top. Stir the food or let it stand a few minutes to even out the heating before you taste it. Taste carefully.

- Use caution when removing lids or other coverings from foods so you can point the steam away from you.

- Read the use-and-care manual before using aluminum foil or metal of any kind in the microwave.

- Never heat food in an unopened bottle or jar in the microwave. Uneven heating and glass that is not made to withstand very hot temperatures can be safety hazards. The glass can break.

- Follow directions on packaged food products carefully, because each manufacturer has special directions for their products.

- Use caution and follow directions carefully when preparing microwave popcorn. Be very careful when opening the bag. The temperature of steam inside the bag can cause painful burns.

- When heating water for hot cocoa mix or soup mix, add the mix to the water before microwaving and stir once or twice. Whenever possible use microwavable glass measuring cups. Their slanted sides help to avoid heating water to a temperature above boiling, which can cause it to jump out of the cup.

- Do not use twist ties on any kind of bag in the microwave. Some contain metal wire which can act as a miniature antenna and cause sparks (arcing).

- Do not use the microwave for deep-fat frying. The oil temperatures are too uneven and the hot oil is too difficult to handle safely.

- Do not microwave raw eggs in the shell or heat whole, peeled cooked eggs in the microwave. They can burst during microwaving.

- Do not overcook foods. Dry foods such as popped popcorn and baked potatoes can catch fire. *If a fire should occur from overcooked food or overheated utensils, leave the door closed and shut off or unplug the microwave.*

Microwave Cooking Magic

Microwave cooking is so quick, it seems almost magical! Microwaves are simply a kind of radiant energy, much like radio and television waves that can't be seen with your eyes. Enclosed in a special box, the microwaves jiggle the water in food so fast that it gets hot enough to cook the food. It's like rubbing your hands together very fast when you want to make them warm. The following facts are helpful to know:

- Microwaves cook best those foods that have moisture, sugar and fat in them.

- Soft foods like muffins will cook faster than hard foods like potatoes, even though they may be the same size.

- Food pieces that are all the same size will cook the most evenly.

- The center of foods will always be the last to cook, so it's best to put foods in a ring shape or with the thickest parts to the outside of the dish.

- The colder the food, the longer it will take to heat or cook.

- The more food you have to cook, the longer it will take.

- It's easy to overcook in the microwave. Always check foods at the shortest cooking time to see if they're done. If not, microwave longer, but check the food often.

Special Ways to Microwave

Stir to help food cook more quickly. Stir from the outside to the middle; food heats faster on the outside.

Turn the dish 1/4 or 1/2 turn to even out the cooking for foods that can't be stirred, such as cakes and lasagne.

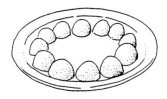

Arrange foods in a circle when there are small pieces like muffins, potatoes and nachos, since the middle is the last to cook.

Cover with the Lid to speed heating by holding in the steam. Be sure the lid knob is easy to handle when using potholders.

Elevate by putting a dinner plate upside down in the middle of the microwave. Put the food to be cooked on top of the dinner plate. This helps the bottom of the food cook better.

Cover with Waxed Paper with the curled side down so it stays on the container better. Otherwise the moving air in the microwave could blow it off. Covering with waxed paper holds in heat and prevents spattering.

Kitchen Computing

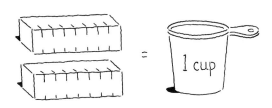

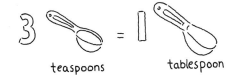

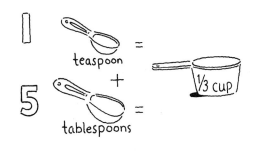

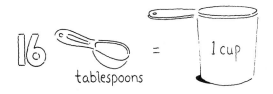

Utensils You Should Have

FOR MEASURING

Rubber scraper

Metal spatula

Liquid measuring cup
(1, 2 and 4 cup)

Measuring spoons
(¼, ½, 1-teaspoon,
1-tablespoon)

Dry measuring cups
(1, ½, ⅓, ¼-cup)

FOR PREPARING

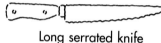
Apple corer

Covered rolling pin

Wire whisk

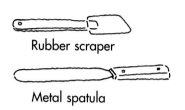
Kitchen scissors

Long serrated knife

Juicer

Sharp knife

Timer

Can opener

Ice-cream scoop

Colander

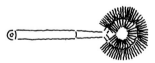
Vegetable peeler

Strainer

Eggbeater

Vegetable brush

Custard cups
(6- and 10-ounce)

Pastry brush

Mixing bowls (set of 3)

Cookie cutter

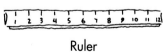
Ruler

Cutting board

Slotted spoon

Tongs

Long-handled fork

Wooden spoon or
Long-handled spoon

Pancake turner

Large saucepan with lid

Round dish

Potholder

Jelly roll pan (15½ × 10½ × 1 inches)

Oblong rectangular pan
(13 inches)

Wire cooling rack

8-inch square dish

9-inch square pan

Loaf pan
(9 × 5 × 3 inches)

Microwaveable mug

Casseroles with lids
(1, 2 or 3 quart)

Microwaveable pan with rack

FOODS	DIRECTIONS	SPEED AND TIME
1 cup water or soup	Pour into microwavable 1 1/2-cup mug. Stir halfway through cooking.	High (100%) 1 to 2 minutes until hot.
1 cup hot chocolate made with cold milk	Pour into microwavable 1 1/2-cup mug. Stir halfway through cooking.	High (100%) 2 to 2 1/2 minutes until hot.
Bacon 1 to 2 slices	Put on microwavable rack in dish or paper towel–lined plate. Cover with paper towels.	High (100%) 45 seconds to 2 minutes until crisp.
4 slices		3 to 4 minutes until crisp.
1 serving S'Mores	Put graham cracker square on napkin. Top with square of milk chocolate candy bar and a large marshmallow.	High (100%) 10 to 15 seconds until puffed. Then top with another cracker square.
1 bowl of spaghetti or chili (about 1 cup)	Put in microwavable bowl. Cover with waxed paper, curled side down, so it doesn't spatter. Stir halfway through cooking.	High (100%) 1 1/2 to 2 1/2 minutes until hot.
1 muffin or roll	Put on napkin or paper towel.	Medium (50%) 15 to 20 seconds until warm.
1 hot dog in a bun	Put hot dog in a bun. Wrap in a napkin or paper towel.	High (100%) 15 to 30 seconds until hot.
1 scrambled egg	In a microwavable 1-cup glass measuring cup, beat 1 egg, 1 tablespoon milk or water and 1 teaspoon margarine or butter with a fork. Stir after 30 seconds.	High (100%) 45 seconds to 1 minute until puffed and firm but still moist. Let stand about 3 minutes.

FOODS	DIRECTIONS	SPEED AND TIME
Corn on the cob 1 ear	Wrap husked ear of corn in waxed paper. Twist the ends. Put on paper towel on a microwavable plate. Use tongs or potholders to turn over halfway through cooking.	High (100%) 2 to 3 minutes until tender. Let stand about 3 minutes.
2 ears		4 to 5 minutes until tender. Let stand about 3 minutes.
Potatoes 1 medium	Scrub, then poke with a fork 2 or 3 times. Put on paper towel on a microwavable plate. Put 4 in a circle. Use tongs or potholders to turn over halfway through cooking.	High (100%) 3 to 4 minutes until soft when poked with a fork. Let stand 5 minutes.
2 medium		5 to 7 minutes
4 medium		11 to 13 minutes

∼∘∼∘∼∘∼∘ MICROWAVING TIPS ∘∼∘∼∘∼∘∼

Margarine or butter, melting	Put in a microwavable custard cup or small bowl.	High (100%)
1 to 2 tablespoons		15 to 30 seconds
3 to 4 tablespoons		30 to 45 seconds
Margarine or butter, softening	Put in a microwavable custard cup or small bowl.	High (100%)
1 to 3 tablespoons		15 to 30 seconds
1/4 to 1 cup		30 to 45 seconds
Chocolate chips, melting	Put in a microwavable measuring cup or small bowl. They will get shiny but won't change their shape.	Medium (50%)
1/2 to 1 cup		3 to 4 minutes
Cream cheese, softening	Put on a microwavable plate.	Medium (50%)
3 ounce package		30 to 40 seconds
8 ounce package		60 to 90 seconds

Table Talk

You can make mealtimes more fun by setting a nice-looking table. The drawing on the right shows you how to set the table correctly. If some pieces aren't needed, such as the cup and saucer, you don't have to put them on the table. If you like, put the napkin in a pretty napkin ring to make the table look really special!

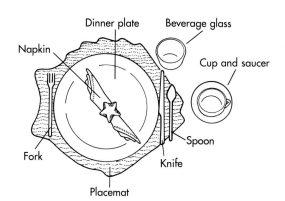

Microwave Dishes

Use containers and plates made of glass, ceramic, plastic or paper. Each recipe will tell you the size needed. Make sure the dishes have handles so they can easily be held when you use potholders. Ask an adult to help you choose the right dishes.

Do Not Use metal pans or any nonmetal dishes with metal trim. Metal can cause sparking and/or damage the dish or the microwave.

If You're Not Sure if a dish can be used in the microwave, ask an adult to help you do the following test:

Put the dish you're not sure about to one side of the middle in the microwave. Fill a glass measuring cup with cool water to the 1-cup line and put it next to the dish. Microwave both on High (100%) 1 minute. If the water in the cup is warm and the dish is cool, the dish can be used for microwaving. If the water stayed at the same temperature and the dish feels warm, the dish should not be used in the microwave.

Cooking and Microwave Words To Know

Arrange: Put food in a special pattern, such as a circle, so it cooks more evenly.

Beat: Make smooth with a quick stirring motion using a spoon, wire whisk, eggbeater or electric mixer.

Boil: Heat liquid until bubbles keep rising and breaking on the surface.

Chop: Cut food into small, uneven pieces; a sharp knife, food chopper or food processor may be used.

Core: Cut out the stem end and remove the seeds.

Drain: Pour off liquid or let it run off through the holes in a strainer or colander, as when draining a can of blueberries. Or, remove pieces of food from a fat or liquid and set them on paper towels to soak up extra moisture.

Grease: Spread the bottom and sides of a dish with butter or shortening.

Mix: Combine to distribute ingredients evenly using a spoon, blender or an electric mixer.

Knead: Curve your fingers and fold dough toward you, then push it away with the heels of your hands, using a quick rocking motion. (See Finger Dough, page 151.)

Let Stand: After taking the food out of the oven, let it sit for the amount of time called for in the recipe.

Peel: Cut off the skin.

Poke: Put a small hole in the skin of a food with a fork or the tip of a sharp knife so steam can get out and it doesn't burst. For example, the skin of a potato or apple.

Sparking (or Arcing): White flashes or sparks with sharp, crackling sounds seen and heard while microwave cooking. It can damage your microwave oven or dishes. To avoid sparking, do not use metal containers, metal twist ties or dishes that have metal trim in your microwave oven.

Toss: Tumble ingredients lightly with a lifting motion, like tossing a salad.

Turn: Move the dish halfway around or 1/4 way around so the food cooks more evenly. Used for foods that can't be stirred.

Whip: Beat rapidly to make light and fluffy, using an electric mixer or eggbeater.

The Right Measure

All-Purpose Flour. Spoon flour lightly into a dry measuring cup. Level with a spatula. Bisquick baking mix and granulated and powdered sugar are measured the same way.

Chopped Nuts or Shredded Cheese. Pack lightly to the top of a dry measuring cup. Also measure soft bread crumbs or shredded coconut this way.

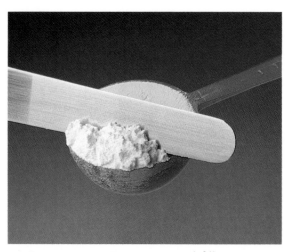

Baking Powder. Dip and fill a measuring spoon. Level with a spatula. Baking soda and spices are measured in the same way. Small amounts of liquids, such as vanilla, can also be measured in measuring spoons.

Brown Sugar. Pack firmly into a dry measuring cup. Level with a spatula or spoon.

Shortening. Pack firmly into a dry measuring cup. Level with a spatula and remove with a rubber scraper.

Molasses and Corn Syrup. Pour into a liquid measuring cup. Remove with a rubber scraper.

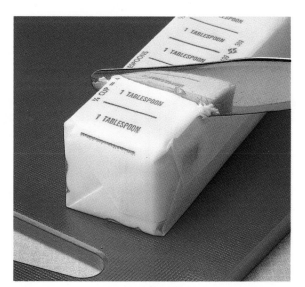

Margarine or Butter. Cut with a table knife right from the refrigerator while it's firm. Use the measurement marks on the wrapper as a guide.

Milk and Other Liquids. Set a liquid measuring cup on the counter. Pour in the liquid. Bend down to check the correct amount at eye level.

LIGHT

SNACKS

AND

HOT

DRINKS

Wobbles

About 24 pieces

INGREDIENTS

Apple, cranapple
  or crangrape juice
Sugar
Any flavor
  unsweetened soft
  drink mix (dry)
Unflavored gelatin

UTENSILS

Microwavable
  4-cup glass
  measuring cup
Dry measuring cups
Spoon
Potholders
13 × 9-inch
  rectangular pan or
  9-inch square pan
Cookie cutters
Pancake turner

1. Pour into the glass measuring cup

> 2 1/2 cups apple, cranapple or
> crangrape juice

2. Stir into the juice until the grains of sugar disappear

> 1 cup sugar
> 1 package (2-quart size) any flavor
> unsweetened soft drink mix (dry)

3. Sprinkle evenly over the juice mixture and let stand for 3 to 4 minutes or until almost all the gelatin is wet

> 4 envelopes unflavored gelatin

4. Microwave uncovered on High (100%) 5 minutes. Carefully stir. Microwave on High (100%) 4 to 6 minutes longer or until boiling. Ask an adult to carefully remove the cup from the microwave.

5. Let stand uncovered about 15 minutes.

6. Put the pan on a counter close to the refrigerator, and ask an adult to pour the hot juice into the pan.

7. Ask an adult to place the pan in the refrigerator. Refrigerate uncovered about 2 hours or until firm.

8. Cut into shapes with your favorite cookie cutters or cut into squares. The first pieces may be difficult to remove from the pan. (Don't worry if a few break.) Carefully lift pieces from the pan with a pancake turner.

HINTS: *If you cut the Wobbles into squares, you will get more pieces. And, if you use a 9-inch square pan, the pieces will be thicker.*

Wobbles

Italian Popcorn

6 cups snack

INGREDIENTS	UTENSILS
Single-serve microwave popcorn	Microwavable 3-quart casserole or bowl
Margarine or butter	Measuring spoons
Italian herb seasoning	Waxed paper
Italian- or cheese-flavored tiny fish-shaped crackers	Potholders
	Dry measuring cups
	Long-handled spoon
Grated Parmesan cheese	Table knife

1. Prepare in the microwave, following the package directions

> 1 package (1.75 ounces) single-serve microwave popcorn

2. Carefully open the bag of popcorn, pointing the opening away from your face to let the steam out.

3. Put in the casserole

> 2 tablespoons margarine or butter
> 1/2 teaspoon Italian herb seasoning

4. Cover with waxed paper, curled side down. Microwave on High (100%) about 30 to 60 seconds or until melted. Carefully lift the edge of waxed paper farthest away from you to let the steam out, then remove the waxed paper.

5. Pour the popcorn into the casserole and add

> 2 cups Italian- or cheese-flavored tiny fish-shaped crackers

6. Toss the mixture to coat evenly.

7. Sprinkle with

> 1 to 2 tablespoons grated Parmesan cheese

8. Toss to coat evenly. Microwave uncovered on High (100%) 1 minute. Stir. Microwave 1 to 2 minutes longer or until toasted.

9. Toss again before serving.

HINT: *If you like, different flavors of fish-shaped crackers may be used. You can also use small crackers of other shapes.*

Brad, *a real food lover, said, "Italian Popcorn was an interesting blend of Italian spices with cheese."*

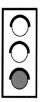

Zoo Snacks

3 cups snack

INGREDIENTS

Margarine or butter
Tiny teddy
  bear-shaped
  cookies
Animal-shaped
  cookies or
  crackers
Dry-roasted
  peanuts
Raisins or chewy
  bite-size fruit
  snacks
Sugar
Ground cinnamon

UTENSILS

Microwavable
  2-quart casserole
  or bowl
Waxed paper
Potholders
Table knife
Long-handled
  spoon
Dry measuring cups
Measuring spoons

1. Put in the casserole

> 2 tablespoons margarine or butter

2. Cover with waxed paper and microwave on High (100%) 30 to 45 seconds or until hot and bubbly. Carefully lift the edge of waxed paper farthest away from you to let the steam out, then remove the waxed paper.

3. Add and toss until well coated

> 1 cup tiny teddy bear-shaped cookies
> 1 cup tiny animal-shaped cookies or crackers
> 1/2 cup dry roasted peanuts

4. Microwave uncovered on High (100%) 1 minute. Stir. Microwave 45 to 60 seconds longer or until toasted.

5. Stir in

> 1/2 cup raisins or chewy bite-size fruit snacks

6. Mix together

> 2 tablespoons sugar
> 1/2 teaspoon ground cinnamon

7. Sprinkle the cinnamon-sugar over the cookie mixture and toss until coated.

8. Let stand uncovered about 5 minutes to cool a little before serving.

HINT: *The waxed paper holds in any splatters from the margarine while you are microwaving the snack. If you use chewy fruit snacks in this mixture, you will need about 3 pouches (.9 ounces each) to make 1/2 cup.*

*After testing Zoo Snacks, **Carrie** told us enthusiastically, "My mom and I like it so much that I've made it three times. I loved this recipe!"*

Jumble Crunch

About 6 cups snack

INGREDIENTS	UTENSILS
Margarine or butter	Microwavable
Chili powder	2-quart casserole
Garlic powder, if	with lid
you like	Dry measuring cups
Toasted oat cereal	Measuring spoons
Corn chips	Potholders
Dry-roasted	Long-handled
peanuts	spoon
Pretzel twists or	Table knife or metal
chips	spatula
	Rubber scraper

1. Put into the casserole

> 1/3 cup margarine or butter
> 1/2 teaspoon chili powder
> 1/4 teaspoon garlic powder

2. Cover with the lid and microwave on High (100%) 30 to 60 seconds or until the margarine is melted. Stir until well mixed.

3. Stir into the margarine mixture and toss until well coated

> 2 cups toasted oat cereal
> 2 cups corn chips
> 1 cup dry-roasted peanuts
> 1 cup small pretzel twists or chips

4. Microwave uncovered on High (100%) 2 minutes. Stir. Microwave 2 to 3 minutes longer or until toasted. Stir.

5. Snack will be hot. Let cool about 30 minutes before eating.

HINT: *If you use the casserole lid, it will keep the margarine from splattering all over the microwave. If you don't have the lid, use a piece of waxed paper, curled side down.*

Maple-Peanut Dip

4 servings

INGREDIENTS	UTENSILS
Peanut butter	Microwavable small
Maple-flavored	bowl
syrup	Rubber scraper
Banana	Dry measuring cups
Apple	Liquid measuring
	cup
	Cutting board
	Sharp knife

1. Mix in the small bowl with the rubber scraper

> 1/2 cup peanut butter
> 1/4 cup maple-flavored syrup

2. Microwave uncovered on High (100%) 15 to 30 seconds or until the mixture is warm and slightly runny.

3. Peel and cut crosswise into 1-inch chunks

1 medium banana

4. Cut into fourths, *then* cut out the core from

1 medium apple

5. Cut apple into bite-size pieces. Dip the fruit pieces into the Maple-Peanut Dip.

Tuna Dip with Veggies

4 servings

INGREDIENTS	UTENSILS
Cream cheese	Microwavable small bowl
Canned tuna in water	Can opener
Carrot	Spoon
Milk	Vegetable peeler
Chopped dried chives	Shredder
Cut-up raw vegetables (cauliflower, broccoli, carrot, celery, zucchini, bell pepper, radishes)	Measuring spoons
	Dry measuring cup
	Cutting board
	Sharp knife

1. Unwrap and put into the small bowl

1 package (3 ounces) cream cheese

2. Microwave uncovered on Medium (50%) 30 to 45 seconds or until softened.

3. Drain and stir into the cream cheese

1 can (3 1/4 ounces) tuna in water

4. Wash, peel, shred and stir into the cream cheese

1 small carrot

5. Stir in

1 tablespoon milk 1 teaspoon chopped dried chives

6. Microwave uncovered on High (100%) 30 seconds. Stir. Microwave 30 to 60 seconds longer or until warm. Use as a dip for

2 cups cut-up raw vegetables

HINTS: *Be sure to use the right size can of tuna. This size usually comes with three little cans in a cardboard "sleeve." An easy way to drain the tuna is to press the opened lid against the tuna in the can, then drain off the liquid into the sink.*

Quick Chili Dip

About 1 1/2 cups dip

INGREDIENTS	UTENSILS
Pasteurized process cheese spread	Spoon
Chopped mild green chilies	Microwavable 1-quart casserole with lid
Canned chili, with or without beans	Can opener
Tortilla chips or raw cut-up vegetables	Measuring spoons
	Potholders

1. Spoon into the casserole

> 1 jar (8 ounces) pasteurized process cheese spread

2. Sprinkle over the cheese

> 1 tablespoon chopped mild green chilies

3. Pour over the cheese and chilies

> 1 can (7 3/8 ounces) chili

Quick Chili Dip, Nifty Nachos (page 29)

4. Cover with the lid and microwave on High (100%) 2 minutes. Stir.

5. Re-cover and microwave on High (100%) 1 to 2 minutes longer or until the cheese is melted and the mixture is hot. Using potholders, carefully remove the casserole from the microwave. Remove the lid, lifting it from the side away from you, to let the steam out.

6. Stir the dip until well blended. Serve with

> Tortilla chips or raw cut-up vegetables

7. Cover and refrigerate any remaining dip for up to 3 days.

HINTS: *If you like, chopped black olives can be substituted for the green chilies. You can find a small can of chili with the single-serving main dishes at your supermarket.*

Ham Snacks

4 servings

INGREDIENTS

Crisp rye crackers
Canned deviled
  ham or chicken
Process American
  cheese

UTENSILS

Microwavable
  dinner plate or
  paper plate
Can opener
Table knife or metal
  spatula
Cutting board

1. Arrange on the plate in a circle

> 4 rectangular crisp rye crackers

2. Divide evenly (about 1 tablespoon per cracker) and spread the crackers with

> 1 can (2 1/4 ounces) deviled ham or chicken

3. Cut in half and place on top of the ham

> 2 slices process American cheese

4. Microwave uncovered on High (100%) about 30 seconds or until the cheese is melted.

HINTS: *If you like mustard, spread a thin layer over the cracker before adding the ham. Deviled ham also comes in a larger size can. If this is the only size you can buy, use 1 tablespoon on each cracker.*

*This delicious snack comes highly recommended by **Melissa.** She commented, "Tastes good—I really love all these ingredients together. It's very cheesy and easy to make."*

Tortilla Roll-up

1 serving

INGREDIENTS

Flour tortilla
Mustard, if you like
Bologna
Process American
  cheese

UTENSILS

Microwavable
  dinner plate or
  paper plate
Table knife or metal
  spatula

1. Put on the plate

> 1 flour tortilla (about 6 inches in diameter)

2. Spread very lightly with

> Mustard

3. Layer on top of the mustard

> 1 slice bologna
> 1 slice process American cheese

4. Roll up the tortilla. Put the rolled tortilla with the open edge down on the plate.

5. Microwave uncovered on High (100%) 15 to 30 seconds or until the cheese is melted.

Tony *gave Tortilla Roll-up high marks. He said, "Easy and quick and you can make it yourself."*

Nifty Nachos

1 serving

INGREDIENTS	UTENSILS
Round tortilla chips	Microwavable
Chopped mild	dinner plate or
green chilies	paper plate
Shredded Monterey	Can opener
Jack or Cheddar	Measuring spoons
cheese	Spoon
	Dry measuring cups

1. Put in a circle on the plate

> 6 round tortilla chips

2. Spoon onto *each* chip

> About 1/2 teaspoon chopped mild green chilies

3. Sprinkle chips evenly with

> 1/4 cup shredded Monterey Jack or Cheddar cheese (1 ounce)

4. Microwave uncovered on High (100%) 20 to 30 seconds or until the cheese is melted.

NACHOS WITH SALSA: Spoon mild salsa on the tortilla chips in place of the chopped green chilies.

Branded Potatoes

4 servings

INGREDIENTS	UTENSILS
Baking potatoes	Paper towels
Liquid browning sauce	Cutting board
	Sharp knife
Margarine or butter	Bottle opener
Garlic salt	Cotton-covered swab
	Microwavable 8-inch round dish
	Table knife
	Measuring spoons
	Potholders
	Fork

1. Ask an adult to help. Do not peel potatoes. Wash and dry with paper towels. Cut in half lengthwise

> 2 medium baking potatoes (about the same size and shape)

2. Using the pointed end of a bottle opener, apple corer, vegetable peeler or the end of a table knife, carefully carve your initials, numbers or other designs in the rounded sides of the potatoes (ask an adult to help).

3. Using a cotton-covered swab, a pastry brush or a very small, clean brush, paint the carved-out part with

> Liquid browning sauce

4. Put into the round dish

> 1 tablespoon margarine or butter

5. Microwave uncovered on High (100%) 15 to 30 seconds or until melted.

6. Sprinkle the flat sides of the potatoes with

> 1/4 teaspoon garlic salt

7. Put potatoes with the flat sides down in a circle in the melted margarine.

8. Microwave uncovered on High (100%) 4 minutes. Turn the dish 1/2 turn. Microwave 2 to 4 minutes longer or until the potatoes are tender when poked with a fork.

9. Let stand uncovered 5 minutes before serving.

HINTS: *If you do not have liquid browning sauce, use molasses (potato may taste a bit sweet). Round, short potatoes will take a little longer to microwave than flat, long potatoes.*

Betsy *had fun branding potatoes. She said, "It was easy and you could carve anything on the potatoes."*

Magnificent Mushrooms

4 servings

INGREDIENTS

Mushrooms
Margarine or butter
Green onion
Dry bread crumbs
Shredded Cheddar
  cheese
Paprika, if you like

UTENSILS

Paper towels
Microwavable small
  bowl
Measuring spoons
Cutting board
Sharp knife
Table knife
Spoon
Microwavable
  dinner plate

1. Carefully wash in cool water and pat dry with paper towels

> 6 large mushrooms (2 to 2 1/2 inches across)

2. Put into the small bowl

> 1 tablespoon margarine or butter

3. Carefully pull out the stems of the mushrooms. Chop enough of the stems to measure 2 tablespoons and add to the margarine in the bowl.

Preceding page: Branded Potatoes (page 30)

4. Wash and chop enough to measure 1 tablespoon, then add to the mushrooms in the bowl

> 1 green onion

5. Microwave uncovered on High (100%) 30 to 60 seconds or until the margarine is melted.

6. Stir in until evenly mixed

> 3 tablespoons dry bread crumbs
> 3 tablespoons shredded Cheddar cheese

7. Spoon about 2 tablespoons of the crumb mixture into the hollow side of each mushroom cap. Pack down a little. Sprinkle with paprika.

8. Put 1 paper towel on the microwavable dinner plate. Arrange the mushrooms with filling sides up in a circle on the paper towel.

9. Microwave uncovered on High (100%) 1 minute. Turn the plate 1/2 turn. Microwave 30 seconds to 1 1/2 minutes longer or until hot. Let stand uncovered about 2 minutes. Be very careful taking your first bite because the moist filling can be hotter than the mushroom cap.

HINTS: *The first tablespoon of filling will pack down into the hollow of the mushroom. The second tablespoon will mound on the top. You can put the mushrooms on a microwavable rack in a microwavable dish instead of on a paper towel on a plate.*

Golden Potato Bites

4 servings

INGREDIENTS	UTENSILS
Frozen potato nuggets	Microwavable paper towels
Shredded Cheddar cheese or Monterey Jack cheese with jalapeño chilies	Microwavable dinner plate
	Dry measuring cups
	Potholders

1. Put 2 paper towels on the plate. Put on the paper towels in a single layer, making a circle

> 2 cups frozen potato nuggets

2. Microwave uncovered on Medium (50%) 3 minutes. Turn the plate 1/2 turn. Microwave on Medium (50%) 2 to 3 minutes longer or until warm.

3. Carefully remove the paper towels by slowly pulling them out so the nuggets roll back onto the plate. Arrange the nuggets close together in a circle again. Sprinkle with

> 1/2 cup shredded Cheddar cheese or Monterey Jack cheese with jalapeño chilies (2 ounces)

4. Microwave uncovered on Medium (50%) 2 to 3 minutes or until the cheese is melted.

Creamy Fruit-topped Bagels

4 servings

INGREDIENTS	UTENSILS
Whipped cream cheese	Small bowl
Strawberry, cherry or apricot jam or jelly	Measuring spoons
Bagels	Spoon
	Cutting board
	Sharp knife
	Microwaveable plate
	Table knife

1. Mix together in the small bowl until well blended

> 1 container (4 ounces) whipped cream cheese
> 2 tablespoons strawberry, cherry or apricot jam or jelly

2. Ask an adult to help. For each serving, split by cutting horizontally in half

> 1 bagel

3. Place bagel on the plate, cut sides up. Spread each half with about 1 tablespoon of the cream cheese spread.

4. Microwave uncovered on High (100%) 20 to 30 seconds or until warm.

5. Cover and refrigerate any remaining cream cheese spread for up to 3 days.

Crunchy Taters

8 snacks

INGREDIENTS	UTENSILS
Corn chips	Plastic bag (1-quart
Margarine or butter	size)
Baking potato	Rolling pin
	Shallow
	microwavable
	cereal bowl
	Table knife
	Measuring spoons
	Paper towel
	Sharp knife
	Cutting board
	Microwavable dish
	with rack
	Potholders

1. Put in the plastic bag and crush with the rolling pin

> 1 package (1 1/2 ounces) corn chips (any flavor)

2. Put in the cereal bowl

> 2 tablespoons margarine or butter

3. Microwave uncovered on High (100%) 15 to 30 seconds or until melted.

4. Wash, pat dry with a paper towel and cut lengthwise into 8 pieces

> 1 large baking potato

5. Dip the potato wedges into margarine, then drop, 1 or 2 at a time, into plastic bag of crushed chips. Put potatoes in 2 rows, about 1 inch apart, on the rack in the dish.

6. Microwave uncovered on High (100%) 5 minutes. Turn the dish 1/2 turn. Microwave 4 to 5 minutes longer or until the potato wedges are tender when poked with a fork.

7. Let stand uncovered about 5 minutes.

HINT: *The bowl for melting the margarine should be as wide as the potato is long. This size bag of corn chips when crushed equals about 1/3 cup of crumbs.*

Golden Potato Bites (bottom), Crunchy Taters (top)

Nutty Banana Pops

8 pops

INGREDIENTS

Chopped peanuts
Bananas
Peanut butter chips,
  semisweet or milk
  chocolate chips
Vegetable oil

UTENSILS

Aluminum foil
Jelly roll pan
Pie plate or waxed
  paper
Dry measuring cups
Table knife
8 flat wooden sticks
  (about 4 inches
  long)
Microwavable
  2-cup glass
  measuring cup
Measuring spoons
Spoon

1. Put a piece of aluminum foil on the jelly roll pan to cover the bottom.

2. Put in the pie plate or on a piece of waxed paper

> 1 1/2 cups chopped peanuts

3. Peel and cut in half crosswise

> 4 medium bananas

4. Push into the cut end of *each* banana

> 1 flat wooden stick

5. Put in the glass measuring cup

> 1 1/2 cups peanut butter chips,
> semisweet or milk chocolate chips
> 2 tablespoons vegetable oil

6. Microwave uncovered on Medium (50%) 3 to 4 minutes or until the chips can be stirred smooth. The chips won't change their shape but they'll look shiny.

7. Dip the banana pops, one at a time, in the peanut butter mixture. Spoon the mixture over the banana if necessary. Roll in the chopped peanuts. Put on the foil-lined pan so they don't touch.

8. Freeze about 2 hours or until firm.

9. Wrap each pop separately in aluminum foil or plastic wrap to store.

HINT: *You can roll the banana pops in other kinds of nuts, rainbow chips or crushed candies if you like. Different kinds of candies and nuts can be used to make fun faces!*

Sometimes great new recipes are created when you experiment with ingredients. **Mike** *told us, "It would be fun to roll these in crispy cereal."*

Nutty Banana Pops, Banana Cookie Bars (page 140)

Caramel Apples

6 apples

INGREDIENTS	UTENSILS
Apples	Paper towels
Granola, chopped peanuts or miniature candy-coated chocolate candies	6 flat wooden sticks (about 4 inches long)
Vanilla caramels	Waxed paper
Water	Measuring spoons
Creamy peanut butter	Microwavable 4-cup glass measuring cup
Ground cinnamon	Dry measuring cups
	Long-handled spoon
	Potholders

1. Wash and dry with paper towels

> 6 medium apples

2. Ask an adult to poke into the stem end of *each* apple

> 1 flat wooden stick

3. Using 1 tablespoon for each mound, make 6 mounds of granola about 3 inches apart on waxed paper, using

> 6 tablespoons granola, chopped peanuts or chopped candy-coated chocolate candies

4. Put in the glass measuring cup

> 1 package (14 ounces) vanilla caramels, wrappers removed
> 2 tablespoons water
> 1/4 cup creamy peanut butter
> 1/2 teaspoon ground cinnamon

5. Microwave uncovered on High (100%) 2 minutes. Stir. Microwave 30 to 60 seconds longer or until the caramels are smooth when stirred. Ask an adult to remove the measuring cup from the microwave.

6. Ask an adult to help. Carefully dip each apple into the hot caramel mixture and spoon the mixture over each apple until it is completely coated. (If caramel thickens, microwave uncovered on High [100%] 30 seconds.)

7. Hold the apple right side up by the stick for a few seconds to let the extra caramel drip off. Then place the apple with the stick side up on one of the mounds of granola. Turn the apple so all of the granola sticks onto it.

8. Refrigerate about 1 hour or until the caramel coating is firm.

CHOCOLATY CARAMEL APPLES: Use 1/4 cup of chocolate chips in place of the peanut butter, and chocolate caramels in place of the vanilla caramels.

My Hot Cocoa

4 servings

INGREDIENTS	UTENSILS
Sugar	Microwavable
Unsweetened cocoa	4-cup glass
Salt	measuring cup
Water	Measuring spoons
Milk	Long-handled
Vanilla, if you like	spoon
	Liquid measuring
	cup
	Potholders
	Mugs or cups

1. Mix in the 4-cup measuring cup

> 3 tablespoons sugar
> 3 tablespoons unsweetened cocoa
> 1/8 teaspoon salt

2. Stir in, a little at a time

> 3/4 cup water

3. Microwave uncovered on High (100%) 1 to 2 minutes or until boiling.

4. Slowly stir in

> 2 1/4 cups milk

5. Microwave uncovered on High (100%) 2 to 3 minutes or until hot (do not boil). Ask an adult to remove the measuring cup from the microwave.

6. Stir in

> 1/4 teaspoon vanilla

7. Ask an adult to carefully pour the hot cocoa into the mugs. Top with marshmallows or whipped cream if you like.

Chilly Day Cinnamon Cider

1 serving

INGREDIENTS	UTENSILS
Apple cider or	Large
apple juice	microwavable
Honey	mug or cup
Pinch of ground	Liquid measuring
cinnamon	cup
	Measuring spoons
	Spoon
	Potholders

1. Pour into the mug

> 1 cup apple cider or apple juice

2. Stir into the cider

> 1 1/2 teaspoons honey
> Pinch of ground cinnamon

3. Microwave uncovered on High (100%) 1 to 2 minutes or until the cider is hot. Stir.

Berry Cloud Float

4 servings

INGREDIENTS

Water
Strawberry-,
  cherry- or
  raspberry-flavored
  gelatin
2 cups vanilla ice
  cream (4 scoops)
Carbonated
  lemon-lime soft
  drink

UTENSILS

Microwavable
  4-cup glass
  measuring cup
Waxed paper
Potholders
Spoon
4 large mugs
Ice cream scoop
Liquid measuring
  cup

1. Measure in the glass measuring cup

1 1/2 cups water

2. Cover with waxed paper, curled side down. Microwave on High (100%) 2 to 3 minutes or until boiling. Using potholders, carefully remove from the microwave. Carefully lift the edge of waxed paper farthest away from you to let the steam out, then remove the waxed paper.

Preceding pages: Italian Popcorn (page 22), Caramel Apples (page 38), My Hot Cocoa (page 39), Chilly Day Cinnamon Cider (page 39)

3. Stir in until completely dissolved

1 package (3 ounces) strawberry-, cherry- or raspberry-flavored gelatin

4. Put into *each* mug

1 scoop vanilla ice cream

5. Divide the strawberry mixture evenly among the mugs.

6. Pour about 1/4 cup over the ice cream in each mug from

1 can (12 ounces) carbonated lemon-lime soft drink

SUNNY CLOUD FLOAT: Use orange-flavored gelatin instead of strawberry gelatin, and carbonated orange soft drink in place of the lemon-lime soft drink.

Rachel loved this snack so much, she named it. She said: "It's like a root beer float, yet it was like fruit punch, and I love mixing fruity things and having them taste good, too!"

Fizzy Chocolate

2 servings

INGREDIENTS

Chocolate syrup
Milk
Carbonated cola or
  lemon-lime soft
  drink

UTENSILS

2 large
  microwavable
  mugs (each holds
  about 1 1/2 cups)
Measuring spoons
Liquid measuring
  cup
Spoon
Potholders

1. Stir together in *each* of the mugs until well blended

> 2 tablespoons chocolate syrup
> 1/2 cup milk

2. Microwave the mugs uncovered on High (100%) 2 to 3 minutes or until the milk is hot.

3. Dividing between the mugs, slowly add

> 1 can (12 ounces) carbonated cola or lemon-lime soft drink, room temperature

4. Serve with whipped cream if you like.

AFTER THE GAME GRUB

Players and fans will be really hungry after the big game! You can be sure that this delicious meal will be snapped up quickly

Nifty Nachos (page 29)
Prairie Dogs (page 58)
Potato salad
Carrot and celery sticks
Chocolate S'more Squares (page 143)
Fizzy Chocolate (left)

HEARTIER

SNACKS

AND

MINI

MEALS

Chicken Nachos (page 49), Pizza Sticks (page 54), Seawiches (page 51)

Robot Snacks

4 servings

INGREDIENTS

Grape jelly
Ketchup
Grated Parmesan
  cheese
Paprika
Canned whole
  potatoes
Longhorn cheese
Smoked sausages
  or hot dogs
Pimiento-stuffed or
  ripe olives or
  canned pineapple
  chunks

UTENSILS

Spoon
Microwavable
  liquid measuring
  cup
Rubber scraper
Waxed paper
Small bowl
Measuring spoons
Can opener
Strainer
Cutting board
Sharp knife
Microwavable
  dinner plates
12 round toothpicks

1. Spoon into liquid measuring cup until it reaches the 1/3-cup line, leveling out with the rubber scraper.

1/3 cup grape jelly

2. Add to reach the 2/3-cup line

1/3 cup ketchup

3. Cover with waxed paper, curled side down, and microwave on High (100%) 1 minute. Stir. Re-cover and microwave 1 to 1 1/2 minutes longer or until the jelly is almost melted. Stir. Save this sauce.

4. Put in the small bowl

2 tablespoons grated Parmesan cheese
1/4 teaspoon paprika

5. Put the strainer in the sink and put in to drain

1 can (16 ounces) small, whole potatoes

6. Choose the 6 largest potatoes and cut them in half.

7. Roll potato halves in the cheese mixture and put with flat sides down in a circle on the dinner plate.

8. On *each* of the 12 round toothpicks, thread

> 1 cube (1/2 inch) longhorn cheese
> 1 tiny smoked sausage or hot dog
> 1 small pimiento-stuffed or ripe olive or canned pineapple chunk

Thread a cheese cube, tiny sausage and olive on a toothpick.

Poke the cheese end into the potato so the toothpick stands straight up.

9. Poke the cheese end of the toothpick into each potato so the toothpick stands straight up. Microwave uncovered on High (100%) 1 minute. Turn the plate 1/2 turn. Microwave 30 to 45 seconds longer or until cheese starts to melt and sausages are hot. Let stand uncovered 1 minute.

10. Serve with the sauce.

HINTS: *Longhorn cheese melts more slowly than other cheeses so it keeps its shape better. If you change the order of the cheese, sausage and olive on the toothpicks, each robot can have a different "personality."*

MOVIE TIME TREATS

Invite some friends over to watch a movie and serve some of these great snacks. Your friends will really be impressed!

Italian Popcorn (page 22)
Jumble Crunch (page 24)
Zoo Snacks (page 23)
Maple Peanut Dip (page 24)
Robot Snacks (left)
Gooey Marshmallow Bars (page 139)
Pecan Marsmallow Drops (page 141)

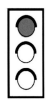

Chicken Logs

4 servings

INGREDIENTS	UTENSILS
Pretzels	Heavy plastic bag (1-quart size)
Margarine or butter	Rolling pin
Boneless, skinless chicken breast halves	Microwavable shallow bowl or pie plate
Taco sauce or sour cream dip	Table knife or metal spatula
	Plastic cutting board
	Sharp knife
	Table fork
	Microwavable dish with rack
	Potholders

1. Put in the plastic bag and carefully crush with the rolling pin

> 1 package (1 5/8 ounces) pretzels

2. Put in the shallow bowl or pie plate

> 3 tablespoons margarine or butter

3. Microwave uncovered on High (100%) 30 to 45 seconds or until melted.

4. Ask an adult to help. Cut lengthwise into strips about 3/4 inch wide

> 2 boneless, skinless chicken breast halves (about 1/2 pound)

5. Dip the chicken strips in the margarine. Turn to coat all sides. Drop strips, 1 or 2 at a time, into the bag of crushed pretzels. Shake a little to coat.

6. Put in 2 rows on the rack in the dish. Microwave uncovered on High (100%) 2 minutes. Turn the dish 1/2 turn. Microwave 1 to 2 minutes longer or until juices of the chicken run clear when the chicken is cut into with a knife (ask an adult to help).

7. Serve with

> Taco sauce or sour cream dip

HINT: *This small bag of pretzels when crushed equals about 1/2 cup of crumbs.*

Chicken Logs taste delicious, and you'll have a good time making them. **Tom** *commented, "It was fun smashing the pretzels."*

Chicken Nachos

4 servings

INGREDIENTS

Shredded or
  chopped cooked
  chicken or turkey
Shredded Monterey
  Jack cheese
Sour cream
Chopped mild
  green chilies
Tomato
Avocado, if you
  like
Lemon juice
Tortilla chips

UTENSILS

Microwavable
  2-quart casserole
  with lid
Long-handled
  spoon
Dry measuring cups
Can opener
Strainer
Rubber scraper
Potholders
Cutting board
Sharp knife
4 serving plates

1. Mix together in the casserole

> 2 cups shredded or chopped cooked
> chicken or turkey (about 10 ounces)
> 1 1/2 cups shredded Monterey Jack
> cheese (6 ounces)
> 1/2 cup sour cream

2. Put the strainer in the sink and put in
to drain

> 1 can (4 ounces) chopped mild green
> chilies

3. Stir the drained chilies into the casserole. Cover with the lid and microwave on Medium (50%) 3 minutes. Stir. Re-cover and microwave 3 minutes. Stir.

4. Re-cover again and microwave on Medium (50%) 2 to 4 minutes or until the cheese is melted and the mixture is hot. Using potholders, carefully remove the casserole from the microwave. Remove the lid, lifting it from the side away from you, to let the steam out.

5. Wash and chop

> 1 medium tomato

6. Peel and slice

> 1 medium avocado

7. So it doesn't turn brown, sprinkle the avocado with

> 2 teaspoons lemon juice

8. Put about 2 cups on each of the plates from

> 1 package (10 1/2 ounces) tortilla
> chips

9. Spoon the chicken mixture over the chips. Top with the tomato and avocado.

10. Serve with salsa if you like.

HINTS: *Enjoy these nachos for a hearty snack, or for dinner with a salad. We use a lower power level so the sour cream doesn't overcook.*

Cheesy Tunawiches

4 servings

INGREDIENTS	UTENSILS
Canned tuna in water	Can opener
	Strainer
Mayonnaise or salad dressing	Medium bowl
	Dry measuring cups
Shredded cheese	Measuring spoons
Chopped dried chives or parsley	Spoon
	Microwavable dish with rack
English muffins	Rubber scraper
Soft margarine or butter	Table knife or metal spatula

1. Put the strainer in the sink and put in to drain

> 1 can (3 1/4 ounces) tuna in water

2. Put the tuna in the bowl and mix in

> 2 tablespoons mayonnaise or salad dressing
> 1/2 cup shredded cheese (2 ounces)
> 2 teaspoons chopped dried chives or parsley

3. Arrange on the rack in the dish

> 2 English muffins, split

4. Spread the cut sides lightly with

> Soft margarine or butter

5. Spread about 3 tablespoons tuna mixture evenly on each of the muffin halves.

6. Microwave uncovered on High (100%) 1 minute. Turn the dish 1/2 turn. Microwave 1 to 1 1/2 minutes longer or until the tuna mixture is warm and the cheese just begins to melt.

7. Add a ripe olive or tomato slice to top off the sandwich if you like.

CHEESY CHICKENWICHES: Use 1 can (5 ounces) chunk chicken in place of tuna.

HINTS: *For a crunchy snack, use rice or popcorn cakes instead of English muffins. The microwave rack will help stop the bottoms of the English muffins from getting soggy.*

Seawiches

4 servings

INGREDIENTS

Cream cheese
Green bell pepper
Soy sauce
Mini rice cakes or
  crisp round
  crackers
Seafood sticks or
  imitation crab legs

UTENSILS

Microwavable small
  bowl
Cutting board
Sharp knife
Measuring spoons
Fork
Table knife or metal
  spatula

1. Unwrap and put into the small bowl

> 1 package (3 ounces) cream cheese

2. Microwave uncovered on Medium (50%) 30 to 45 seconds or until softened.

3. Wash and chop enough bell pepper to measure 2 tablespoons from

> 1 small green bell pepper

4. Stir the chopped bell pepper into the cream cheese with a fork along with

> 1/2 teaspoon soy sauce

5. Spread the cream cheese mixture on

> 16 mini rice cakes or crisp round crackers '

6. Cut crosswise into 1/2-inch pieces

> 5 seafood sticks or imitation crab legs

7. Put 3 pieces seafood sticks on each cracker.

HINTS: *If the seafood sticks are frozen, cut them before they thaw out—it's easier. Mini rice cakes come in many flavors; you'll find that teriyaki and sesame are especially good with this recipe.*

Little Lunch Pizzas

1 serving

INGREDIENTS

English muffin
Pizza sauce
Shredded Cheddar
  or mozzarella
  cheese

UTENSILS

Toaster
Measuring spoons
Table knife or metal
  spatula
Microwavable
  paper towel
Microwavable
  dinner plate or
  paper plate

1. Toast on medium toaster setting

> 1 English muffin, split

2. Top each muffin half with

> 1 tablespoon pizza sauce
> 1 tablespoon shredded Cheddar or
> mozzarella cheese

3. Put the paper towel on the plate. Put the muffin halves on the paper towel.

4. Microwave uncovered on High (100%) 30 to 45 seconds until the cheese is melted.

5. Cool about 2 minutes before eating.

HINT: *For a heartier pizza, try adding some sliced olives, crumbled cooked hamburger, chopped tomato, sliced pepperoni or other toppings.*

AFTERNOON SNACKS

Try these snacks for after-school treats—they're easy, quick and delicious.

Tortilla Roll-Up (page 28)
Tuna Dip with Veggies (page 25)
Ham Snacks (page 28)
Little Lunch Pizzas (left)

Little Lunch Pizzas

Pizza Sticks

2 servings

INGREDIENTS

Breadsticks or
 bagel sticks
Pizza sauce
Thin-sliced
 pepperoni
String cheese

UTENSILS

Sharp knife
Cutting board
Table knife or metal
 spatula
Measuring spoons
Microwavable dish
 with rack
Microwavable
 paper towel

1. Cut lengthwise in half but not completely through

2 soft breadsticks or bagel sticks

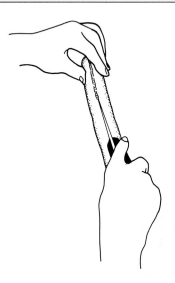

2. Spread on the cut side of each breadstick

1 tablespoon pizza sauce

3. Arrange on 1 side of *each* breadstick, overlapping a little

5 pieces thin-sliced pepperoni

4. Tear lengthwise in half and put on top of the pepperoni

1 stick of string cheese

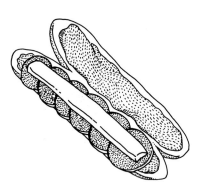

5. Close the breadsticks. Put on the rack in the dish. Cover with the paper towel. Microwave on High (100%) 15 to 45 seconds or until warm.

HINTS: *The softer the breadstick, the faster the cheese melts. If your breadstick is short, you may need only 4 slices of pepperoni. If it is long, you may need 6 slices.*

Bean Burgers

4 open-face burgers

INGREDIENTS

Hamburger buns
Mayonnaise or
  salad dressing
Canned pork and
  beans
Process American
  cheese

UTENSILS

Microwavable dish
  with rack
Table knife or metal
  spatula
Can opener
Spoon

1. Arrange with the cut sides up on the rack in the dish

> 2 sliced hamburger buns

2. Spread the cut sides of the buns lightly with

> Mayonnaise or salad dressing

3. Divide evenly between the buns

> 1 can (8 ounces) pork and beans

4. Top *each* bun half with

> 1 slice process American cheese

5. Microwave uncovered on High (100%) 30 seconds. Turn the dish 1/2 turn. Microwave 30 seconds to 1 minute longer or until the cheese is melted.

HINTS: *Use a different kind of cheese such as nacho or Swiss if you like. Canned baked beans vary, so if they're especially juicy, drain off some of the liquid.*

Bean Burritos

6 burritos

INGREDIENTS

Canned refried beans

Flour tortillas

Shredded Monterey Jack cheese

Fresh cilantro, if you like

Taco sauce, salsa, sour cream or guacamole if you like

UTENSILS

Can opener

Measuring spoons

Table knife or metal spatula

Dry measuring cup

Cutting board

Sharp knife

2 microwavable dinner plates

Waxed paper

Potholders

1. Spread about 3 tablespoons beans over each tortilla almost to the edge

> 1 can (8 ounces) refried beans
> 6 flour tortillas (6 inches in diameter)

2. Sprinkle *each* tortilla with about

> 2 tablespoons shredded Monterey Jack cheese

3. Wash and chop the cilantro into tiny pieces (2 tablespoons). Sprinkle over each tortilla

> 1 teaspoon chopped fresh cilantro

4. Fold 1 end of each tortilla up about 1 inch over the mixture. Fold the right and left sides over the folded end, overlapping. Fold the remaining end up. Place the tortillas with the seam or folded sides down in a circle on each of 2 plates.

5. Cover each plate with waxed paper, curled side down. Microwave 1 plate at a time on High (100%) 2 to 3 minutes or until hot. Carefully lift the edge of waxed paper farthest away from you to let the steam out, then remove the waxed paper.

6. Carefully cut each burrito in half with a sharp knife. Serve with taco sauce, sour cream or guacamole if you like.

HINT: *Cilantro looks very much like parsley and is often called Mexican or Italian parsley. It has a special refreshing, cool, slightly sweet flavor and goes well with Mexican foods. You can use both the stems and leaves.*

Mike suggested, "You should have a sauce or chili with these burritos." We liked his idea so much that we added taco sauce to the recipe.

Bean Burritos, Terrific Tacos (page 62)

Prairie Dogs

4 servings

INGREDIENTS

Mustard or ketchup
Hot dog buns
Hot dogs
Pickle relish,
  shredded cheese,
  chopped onion or
  sauerkraut

UTENSILS

Table knife or metal
  spatula
Cutting board
Sharp knife
Measuring spoons
4 microwavable
  paper napkins
Microwavable
  dinner plate

1. Spread mustard or ketchup lightly on the cut sides of

> 4 sliced hotdog buns.

2. Cut in half lengthwise but not completely through

> 4 hot dogs

3. Spread the hot dogs open slightly and fill *each* with

> 1 tablespoon drained pickle relish, shredded cheese, chopped onion or sauerkraut

Cut hot dogs in half lengthwise, but not completely through. Spread the hot dogs open slightly and fill.

4. Put 1 filled hot dog into *each* bun, making sure the filling is next to the fold.

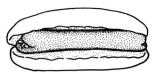

5. Close the bun. Roll each bun up in a paper napkin, folding the ends in as you roll it up.

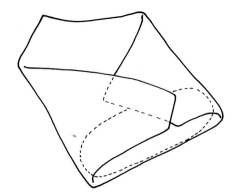

6. Arrange the hot dogs in a circle on the plate. Microwave on High (100%) 1 1/2 to 2 1/2 minutes or until hot.

7. Let stand, still wrapped, about 2 minutes before eating to even out the heat.

8. Unwrap and take your first bite very carefully—it may still be quite hot!

HINTS: *Use hot dog buns that are not cut all the way through. If it seems that the hot dog buns become tough, try using frozen buns with the hot dogs, and that will be less likely to happen.*

*You can be proud when you make a delicious meal for your family. **Eric** enjoyed preparing this recipe; he said, "It's good. I made it myself and I like that. I like stuffing it!"*

*We really like what **Erin** had to say about the Hidden Chicken Pockets on the next page: "It's a good meal to have on a hot night. It was fun preparing all the different toppings. I would put the onions as a topping instead of mixed with the chicken." We thought that was a good suggestion so we changed the recipe!*

Following page: Hidden Chicken Pockets

BEND WINGTIPS UP FOR HIGHER FLIGHTS
BEND WINGTIPS DOWN FOR LOWER FLIGHTS

Hidden Chicken Pockets

8 pockets

INGREDIENTS	UTENSILS
Pita breads	Cutting board
Chopped cooked chicken or turkey	Sharp knife
Vegetable oil	Dry measuring cups
Salt	Measuring spoons
Canned chopped green chilies	Microwavable 1 1/2-quart casserole with lid
Lettuce	Can opener
Onion, if you like	Strainer
Shredded Monterey Jack or Cheddar cheese	Long-handled spoon
Sour cream	Potholders
Taco sauce	

1. Ask an adult to help you carefully split by cutting each *halfway* around the edge with a knife to form a pocket

> 8 pita breads (about 3 1/2 inches in diameter)

2. Mix together in the casserole

> 2 cups chopped cooked chicken or turkey (about 10 ounces)
> 1 tablespoon vegetable oil
> 1/2 teaspoon salt

3. Put the strainer in the sink and put in to drain

> 1 can (4 ounces) chopped green chilies

4. Stir the drained chilies into the mixture. Cover with the lid and microwave on High (100%) 2 minutes. Stir. Re-cover and microwave 2 to 3 minutes or until the chicken is hot. Using potholders, remove the casserole from the microwave. Carefully remove the lid, lifting from the side away from you to let the steam out.

5. Wash and shred (or cut thinly using a sharp knife) enough lettuce to equal 1 cup from

> 1 small head lettuce

6. Peel and chop

> 1 small onion

7. Spoon about 1/4 cup of the chicken mixture into each pita bread. Top *each* with

> 1/4 cup shredded Monterey Jack or Cheddar cheese (8 ounces)
> Shredded lettuce
> About 2 tablespoons chopped onion

8. Serve with

> 1/2 cup sour cream
> 1/2 cup taco sauce

Terrific Tacos

8 tacos

INGREDIENTS	UTENSILS
Tomato	Cutting board
Lettuce	Sharp knife
Hamburger meat or ground turkey	Dry measuring cups
	Measuring spoons
Mild taco sauce	Microwavable
Flour tortillas	2-quart casserole
Shredded Cheddar cheese	with lid
	Long-handled spoon
	Strainer
	Potholders

1. Wash and chop

1 medium tomato

2. Wash and shred (or cut thinly, using a sharp knife) enough lettuce to measure 2 cups from

1 small head lettuce

3. With your fingers, crumble into small pieces into the casserole

1 pound hamburger meat or ground turkey

4. Cover with the lid and microwave on High (100%) 3 minutes. Stir. Re-cover and microwave 2 to 3 minutes longer or until no longer pink.

5. Put the strainer over a container to hold any fat from the meat. Ask an adult to pour the meat carefully into the strainer. Hot steam will rise so be careful. Put the drained meat back into the casserole.

6. Stir into the cooked meat

1 jar (8 ounces) mild taco sauce

7. Cover with the lid and microwave on High (100%) 1 to 2 minutes or until hot. Using potholders, carefully remove the casserole from the microwave. Remove the lid, lifting it from the side away from you, to let the steam out. Stir.

8. Cover and let stand 5 minutes to blend the flavors.

9. Spoon about 1/4 cup taco mixture down the center of *each* of

8 flour tortillas (8 inches in diameter)

10. Sprinkle *each* with about 1/4 cup lettuce, 1 tablespoon chopped tomatoes and

2 tablespoons shredded Cheddar cheese

11. Roll up the tortillas. Serve with additional taco sauce if you like.

Easy Sloppy Joes

6 sandwiches

INGREDIENTS	UTENSILS
Ground turkey or hamburger meat	Microwavable 2-quart casserole with lid
Onion	Cutting board
Worcestershire sauce	Sharp knife
Red pepper sauce	Waxed paper
Canned condensed tomato soup	Long-handled spoon
Hamburger buns	Potholders
	Colander
	Measuring spoons
	Can opener
	Rubber scraper

1. With your fingers, crumble into small pieces into the casserole

> 1 pound ground turkey or hamburger meat

2. Peel, chop and sprinkle over the turkey

> 1 medium onion

3. Cover with waxed paper and microwave on High (100%) 3 minutes. Stir to break up the meat. Re-cover and microwave 3 to 4 minutes longer or until the meat is no longer pink. Using potholders, carefully remove the casserole from the microwave. Carefully lift the edge of waxed paper farthest away from you to let the steam out, then remove the waxed paper.

4. Put the colander over a container to hold any fat from the meat. Ask an adult to pour the meat carefully into the colander.

5. Put the drained meat back into the same casserole. Stir in

> 2 teaspoons Worcestershire sauce
> 3 drops red pepper sauce
> 1 can (10 3/4 ounces) condensed tomato soup

6. Cover with the lid and Microwave on High (100%) 3 minutes. Stir. Recover and microwave 1 to 3 minutes longer or until hot. Using potholders, carefully remove the casserole from the microwave. Remove the lid, lifting it from the side away from you, to let the steam out.

7. Fill with turkey mixture

> 6 sliced hamburger buns

HINT: *If you love cheeseburgers, try a slice of American cheese on top of your Sloppy Joe.*

Hot Heros

2 servings

INGREDIENTS

Hoagie buns
Soft margarine or
  butter
Mayonnaise, if you
  like
Mustard, if you like
Bologna
Cheese
Salami

UTENSILS

Cutting board
Sharp serrated
  knife
Microwavable dish
  with rack
Table knife or metal
  spatula

1. Cut in half lengthwise and put with the cut sides up on the rack

> 2 small hoagie buns (about 6 inches long)

2. Spread each bun half lightly with

> Soft margarine or butter

3. Spread lightly with

> Mayonnaise
> Mustard

4. Cut in half

> 2 slices bologna
> 2 slices cheese
> 2 slices salami

5. Put 2 half slices of bologna on the bottom half of each bun, overlapping the slices so they fit. Put the cheese on next the same way, then the salami.

6. Cover each sandwich with the top half of the bun.

7. Microwave uncovered on Medium (50%) 1 1/2 to 2 1/2 minutes or until the center of the sandwich is warm and the cheese just begins to melt.

HINTS: *Putting the cheese between the two kinds of cold cuts helps to warm the meat before the cheese melts. For extra crunch, add lettuce and/or tomato after microwaving.*

Hot Heros, Robot Snacks (page 46)

MORNING WAKE-UP CALLS

Breakfast-on-a-Plate (page 68), Blueberry Coffee Cake (page 82)

Breakfast Tostada

1 serving

INGREDIENTS

Scrambled Egg
(page 12)
Tostada shell
Taco sauce or salsa
Shredded cheese

UTENSILS

Microwavable
dinner plate
Measuring spoons

1. Follow the recipe on page 12 to cook the Scrambled Egg.

2. Put on the dinner plate

> 1 tostada shell

3. Microwave uncovered on High (100%) 20 to 30 seconds or until hot.

4. Put the scrambled egg on the tostada shell.

5. Top the egg with

> 1 to 2 tablespoons taco sauce or salsa
> 2 tablespoons shredded cheese

HINTS: *You can use mild or hot taco sauce or salsa and any kind of cheese in this recipe.*

Breakfast-on-a-Plate

1 serving

INGREDIENTS

Bacon
Soft margarine or
butter
Egg
Milk
Salt and pepper, if
you like
Chocolate-flavored
syrup

UTENSILS

Microwavable
paper towels
Microwavable
dinner plate
Pastry brush or
waxed paper
Microwavable
6-ounce custard
cup
Fork
Waxed paper
Large microwavable
mug (holds about
1 1/2 cups)
Liquid measuring
cup
Measuring spoons
Spoon
Potholders

1. Put 1 paper towel on the plate. On 1 edge of the paper towel put

> 1 slice bacon

2. Fold one more paper towel in half the long way. Fold again and put over the bacon.

3. Using a pastry brush or a small piece of waxed paper, grease the custard cup with margarine. Break into the cup

1 egg

4. Add and stir with a fork until yellow and white of egg are partly mixed together

2 tablespoons milk Salt and pepper

5. Cover the custard cup with a small piece of waxed paper, curled side down. Put the cup next to the bacon on the plate.

6. Mix in the mug so it's no more than 3/4 full

3/4 cup milk 2 tablespoons chocolate-flavored syrup

7. Put the mug next to the mustard cup.

8. Carefully put the plate of food in the center of the microwave. Don't tip it.

9. Microwave on High (100%) 2 to 4 minutes or until the egg is cooked, the bacon is crisp and the cocoa is hot enough to drink. Carefully remove the plate from the microwave.

10. To remove the waxed paper from the mug, carefully lift the edge of waxed paper farthest away from you to let the steam out, then remove the waxed paper.

We think you'll like this breakfast because it's delicious, fast and easy to clean up! **Murad** *proudly told us, "I made my own hot breakfast today."*

SLEEPOVER SPECIALS

Overnighters with friends mean lots of fun and lots of food! Here are some ideas for round-the-clock recipes.

Fun-To-Make at Night

Branded Potatoes (page 30)
Pizza Sticks (page 54)
Finger Dough (page 151)
Launching Rocket Cones (page 148)

For Breakfast in the Morning

Orange juice
Mix-'em-Up Scrambled Eggs (page 70)
Blueberry Coffee Cake (page 82)
Milk

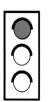

Mix-'Em-Up Scrambled Eggs

4 servings

INGREDIENTS	UTENSILS
Tomato	Sharp knife
Eggs	Cutting board
Salt	Microwavable
Dash of pepper	1-quart casserole
Shredded Cheddar	with lid
cheese	Fork or wire whisk
	Measuring spoons
	Dry measuring cup
	Potholders

1. Wash and chop into 1/2-inch pieces

> 1 medium tomato

2. Beat in the casserole with a fork until well blended

> 4 eggs
> 1/4 teaspoon salt
> Dash of pepper

3. Stir into egg mixture the tomato and

> 1/2 cup shredded Cheddar cheese (2 ounces)

4. Cover the casserole with the lid and microwave on High (100%) 1 minute. Carefully remove the lid. Stir the eggs with the fork or wire wisk.

5. Re-cover. Continue to microwave on High (100%) about 3 minutes longer, stirring after every minute, until eggs are slightly firm but not runny. Using potholders, carefully remove the casserole from the microwave. Remove the lid, lifting it away from you, to let the steam out.

HINT: *Instead of the tomato, add 1 small stalk celery, or 1 small green bell pepper, washed and chopped. Add 1/4 cup milk.*

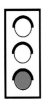

Jelly Bread

1 serving

INGREDIENTS

Egg
Milk
Day-old bread
(white, whole
wheat or
cinnamon)
Jelly or jam (your
favorite flavor)

UTENSILS

Cereal bowl
Fork or eggbeater
Measuring spoons
Large cookie cutter
Microwavable
dinner plate
Spoon

1. Beat in the cereal bowl with the fork or eggbeater until well blended

> 1 egg
> 1 tablespoon milk

2. Cut with a large cookie cutter into an interesting shape

> 1 slice day-old bread (white, whole wheat or cinnamon)

3. Dip the bread into the egg mixture, turning until evenly coated (most of the egg mixture should soak into the bread).

4. Put the egg-coated bread on the plate.

5. Stir with a spoon to soften, then drop onto the bread in a stream to make a fun design

> 1 tablespoon jelly or jam, your favorite flavor

6. Microwave uncovered on High (100%) 1 to 1 1/2 minutes or until the egg looks firm.

7. Let stand uncovered 1 minute.

HINTS: *Be careful taking your first bite—jelly and jam can get really hot! Jam that comes in a squeeze bottle is easy to use in this recipe. Syrup or honey can be used in place of the jam.*

Following pages: Jelly Bread, Mix-'Em-Up Scrambled Eggs (page 70)

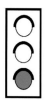

French Toast Sandwich

1 serving

INGREDIENTS

Frozen French toast
Peanut butter
Raisins or chocolate
  chips

UTENSILS

Microwavable plate
Table knife or metal
  spatula
Measuring spoons

1. Put on the plate

1 slice frozen French toast

2. Spread with

1 tablespoon peanut butter

3. Sprinkle the peanut butter with

About 1 tablespoon raisins or chocolate chips

4. Cover the raisins with

1 slice frozen French toast

5. Microwave uncovered on High (100%) 1 1/2 to 2 minutes or until the peanut butter is slightly melted.

6. Let stand 1 minute.

HINT: *Take your first bite carefully—the peanut butter may be very hot! You can use a little less peanut butter and raisins if you like.*

These breakfast sandwiches are delicious and easy, and they're different, too. **Alisha** *told us, "I'd make this recipe again because it's creative."*

Apple Pig Rollers

1 serving

INGREDIENTS

Frozen (thawed)
  microwave
  pancakes or
  leftover pancakes
Applesauce
Frozen, thawed
  microwave pork
  sausage links

UTENSILS

Microwavable
  dinner plate
Table knife or metal
  spatula
Measuring spoons
Toothpicks

1. Put on the plate

> 2 frozen (thawed) microwave pancakes
> or leftover pancakes

2. Spread over each pancake

> 1 tablespoon applesauce

3. Put on 1 end of *each* pancake.

> 1 frozen (thawed) microwave pork
> sausage link

4. Roll up pancakes. Push 2 toothpicks crisscross through each pancake to hold them together. Put the rolled-up pancakes with seam sides down on the plate.

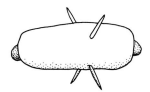

5. Microwave uncovered on High (100%) 1 to 2 minutes or until hot. Let stand 1 minute. Remove the toothpicks before serving. Serve with extra applesauce or syrup if you like.

HINT: *Follow the package directions for thawing microwave pancakes and sausages. Sprinkle the applesauce with cinnamon before rolling the pancake around the sausage.*

*We want to thank **Tony** for the terrific name he gave this recipe. He said, "The recipe was easy and fun."*

Brown-sugared Apples

4 apples

INGREDIENTS

Cooking apples*
Brown sugar
Margarine or butter
Dash of apple pie
   spice or cinnamon
Water

UTENSILS

Paper towels
Apple corer
Small sharp knife
4 microwavable
   small dishes or
      10-ounce custard
      cups
Spoon
Table knife or metal
   spatula
Measuring spoons
Waxed paper
Potholders
Fork

1. Wash and dry with paper towels

> 4 cooking apples

2. Ask an adult to remove the cores from the apples. With small sharp knife, make a very shallow cut all around the middle of the apple. (Cut only the skin of the apple. This will keep the apple from falling apart during cooking.)

3. Put the apples in the small dishes.

4. Fill the center of each apple with

> Brown sugar

5. Put on top of each apple

> 1 teaspoon margarine or butter

6. Sprinkle with

> Apple pie spice or cinnamon

7. Pour into *each* dish

> 1 tablespoon water

8. Arrange the dishes in a square in the microwave. Cover the dishes with one big piece of waxed paper, curled side down.

9. Microwave on High (100%) 4 minutes. Using potholders, carefully turn each dish 1/2 turn.

10. Re-cover and microwave on High (100%) 2 to 6 minutes longer or until the apples are tender when poked with a fork. Carefully lift the edge of waxed paper farthest away from you to let the steam out before you test the apples with a fork. Ask an adult to remove the dishes from the microwave.

11. Let the apples stand uncovered 10 to 15 minutes before eating, because they will be very hot.

* Choose from these varieties of cooking apples: Rome Beauty, Golden Delicious or Greening.

Right: Apple-Pig Rollers (page 74), Brown-sugared Apples; Following page: Berry Muffins (page 79), RasinBran Muffins (page 80)

Berry Muffins

12 muffins

INGREDIENTS	UTENSILS
Margarine or butter	12 paper baking cups
Plain yogurt	Microwavable
Vanilla	6-cup muffin ring
Egg	Microwavable
All-purpose flour	medium bowl
Sugar	Table knife
Baking powder	Spoon
Baking soda	Dry measuring cups
Fresh or frozen	Measuring spoons
cranberries or	Small bowl
blueberries	Cutting board
Sugar	Sharp knife
Ground nutmeg or	Rubber scraper
cinnamon, if you	Potholders
like	Wire cooling rack

1. Put 6 paper baking cups in the micro-wavable muffin ring.

2. Put in the medium bowl

> 3 tablespoons margarine or butter

3. Microwave uncovered on High (100%) about 1 minute or until melted.

4. Add and beat with a spoon

> 1 cup plain yogurt
> 1/2 teaspoon vanilla
> 1 egg

5. Mix together in the small bowl

> 1 1/2 cups all-purpose flour
> 1/4 cup sugar
> 1 teaspoon baking powder
> 1 teaspoon baking soda

6. Stir the flour mixture into the egg mixture all at once, just until the flour is moistened (batter will be lumpy).

7. Ask an adult to chop coarsely to make 2/3 cup

> About 1 cup fresh or frozen cranberries or 2/3 cup blueberries

8. Using rubber scraper, fold the cranberries into the batter. Spoon half of the batter into the 6 baking cups, filling each 3/4 full. Sprinkle with

> 2 teaspoons sugar
> Ground nutmeg or cinnamon

9. Microwave uncovered on High (100%) 1 minute. Turn the ring 1/2 turn.

10. Continue to microwave uncovered on High (100%) 1 to 2 minutes longer or until the tops are almost dry. Using potholders, remove the muffin ring from the microwave.

11. Let muffins stand uncovered in the ring 1 minute, then carefully remove the muffins from the ring and let stand uncovered on cooling rack 2 minutes.

12. Repeat with the remaining paper baking cups, batter, sugar and nutmeg.

Raisin-Bran Muffins

8 muffins

INGREDIENTS

Shreds of wheat
  bran cereal
Milk
All-purpose flour
Raisins
Packed brown
  sugar
Margarine or butter
Baking powder
Salt
Egg

UTENSILS

16 paper baking
  cups
Microwavable
  6-cup muffin ring
Dry measuring cups
Plastic bag
Rolling pin
Medium bowl
Large spoon
Liquid measuring
  cup
Measuring spoons
Spoon
Toothpick
Potholders
Wire cooling rack

1. Put 2 paper baking cups in each of 4 cups opposite each other in the microwavable 6-cup muffin ring.

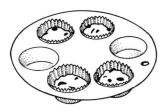

2. Put in the plastic bag and crush with the rolling pin

> 1 cup shreds of wheat bran cereal

3. Mix together in the medium bowl the crushed cereal and

> 2/3 cup milk

4. Let stand about 8 minutes or until the cereal is slightly softened.

5. Stir in just until the flour is moistened (batter will be lumpy)

> 2/3 cup all-purpose flour
> 1/2 cup raisins
> 1/4 cup packed brown sugar
> 1/4 cup margarine or butter
> 1 1/2 teaspoons baking powder
> 1/4 teaspoon salt
> 1 egg

6. Spoon half of the batter into the 4 baking cups, filling each 1/2 full.

7. Microwave uncovered on High (100%) 1 minute. Turn the ring 1/4 turn.

8. Continue to microwave uncovered on High (100%) 1 minute at a time, turning the ring 1/4 turn every minute, until the tops of the muffins are almost dry and a toothpick poked in the centers comes out clean. (Parts of the muffins will look a little wet, but will continue cooking while they stand.) Using potholders, remove the muffin ring from the microwave.

9. Let muffins stand uncovered in the ring 1 minute, then carefully remove the muffins from the ring and let stand uncovered on cooling rack 2 minutes.

10. Repeat with the remaining paper baking cups and batter.

Maple Apples

4 apples

INGREDIENTS

Cooking apples*
Maple-flavored
 syrup
Ground cinnamon

UTENSILS

Paper towels
Cutting board
Sharp knife
Microwavable
 2-quart casserole
 with lid
Liquid measuring
 cup
Measuring spoons
Fork
Potholders
Spoon

1. Wash and dry with paper towels

> 3 medium cooking apples

2. Ask an adult to cut each apple into fourths, then remove the cores. Cut each piece of apple in half lengthwise, then again crosswise to make chunks. Put the apples in the casserole.

3. Pour over the apples

> 1/2 cup maple-flavored syrup

4. Sprinkle with

> 1/4 teaspoon ground cinnamon

5. Cover with the lid and microwave on High (100%) 3 minutes. Stir. Re-cover and microwave 2 to 3 minutes longer or until the apples are tender when poked with a fork. Using potholders, carefully remove the casserole from the microwave. Remove the lid, lifting it from the side away from you to let the steam out.

6. Let the apples stand covered 10 minutes before serving because they will be very hot.

HINTS: *A combination apple corer-and-cutter makes fixing the apples easy. If yours cuts the apples into 12 wedges instead of 8, cut down the microwave time by 1 minute.*

* Choose from these varieties of cooking apples: Rome Beauty, Golden Delicious or Greening.

Autumn Oatmeal

1 serving

INGREDIENTS

Quick-cooking oats
Apple juice or
  apple cider
Chewy bite-size
  fruit snacks (any
  flavor and shape)
Milk

UTENSILS

Large
  microwavable
  mug (holds about
  1 1/2 cups)
Dry measuring cups
Liquid measuring
  cup
Spoon
Potholders

1. Put in the mug

> 1/3 cup quick-cooking oats

2. Stir into the oats until well blended

> 3/4 cup apple juice or apple cider

3. Microwave uncovered on High
(100%) 1 minute. Stir. Microwave 1/2 to
1 1/2 minutes longer or until thickened
when stirred.

4. Stir into the oatmeal

> 1 pouch (about 3/4 ounce) chewy
> bite-size fruit snacks (any flavor and
> shape)

5. Let stand uncovered 1 minute before
serving.

6. Serve with

> Milk

HINT: *You can use fruit punch or other favorite fruit juices in place of the apple juice, but the color of the oatmeal
may change.*

 # Blueberry Coffee Cake

8 servings

INGREDIENTS

Wild blueberry
  muffin mix
Uncrushed
  cornflakes
Packed brown
  sugar
Ground cinnamon
Blueberry, lemon,
  vanilla or plain
  yogurt
Egg
Milk

UTENSILS

Can opener
Strainer
Small bowl
Spoon
Dry measuring cups
Measuring spoons
Long-handled
  spoon
Medium bowl
Liquid measuring
  cup
Rubber scraper
Microwavable
  8-inch round dish
Microwavable
  dinner plate
Toothpick
Potholders

1. Put the strainer in the sink, pour in to drain, then rinse and set aside the blueberries from

> 1 package (13 ounces) wild blueberry muffin mix

2. Crush with the back of a spoon in the small bowl

> 1/2 cup uncrushed cornflakes

3. Stir in until mixed and save

> 2 tablespoons packed brown sugar
> 1/4 teaspoon ground cinnamon

4. Mix together in the medium bowl until blended

> 1/2 cup blueberry, lemon, vanilla, or plain yogurt
> 1 egg

5. Slowly stir in until smooth

> 1/4 cup milk

6. Stir in the muffin mix just until moistened. Spread the batter in the round dish. Sprinkle with the drained blueberries and then the cereal mixture.

7. Put a microwavable dinner plate upside down in microwave. Put the round dish on top of the plate.

8. Microwave uncovered on High (100%) 2 minutes. Turn the dish 1/2 turn. Microwave 3 to 4 minutes longer or until a toothpick poked in several places comes out clean. Using potholders, remove the dish from the microwave.

9. Let stand on a flat, heatproof surface (not wire rack) 10 minutes.

HINT: *If you want to add a frosting to this breakfast treat, it's easy when you use ready-to-spread frosting. Put 2 tablespoons frosting in a microwavable glass measuring cup. Microwave uncovered on High (100%) 10 to 15 seconds or until it can be stirred smooth. Using a spoon, drop the frosting in a stream onto the coffee cake while the cake is warm.*

*This treat comes highly recommended by **Leslie**. She enthusiastically advised, "It was good! Try it!"*

HELPING WITH DINNER

Italian Chicken and Spaghetti (page 90), Garlic Bread (page 119)

Golden Chicken

6 servings

INGREDIENTS

Bisquick® baking
  mix
Paprika
Salt
Pepper
Broiler-fryer
  chicken, cut into
  pieces

UTENSILS

Heavy plastic bag
  (1-gallon size)
Dry measuring cups
Measuring spoons
Microwavable
  rectangular
  baking dish,
  11 × 7 1/2 × 1 1/2
  inches
Waxed paper
Tongs
Potholders
Sharp knife

1. Shake in the plastic bag until well mixed

> 2/3 cup Bisquick baking mix
> 1 1/2 teaspoons paprika
> 1/4 teaspoon salt
> 1/4 teaspoon pepper

2. Shake 1 piece at a time in the plastic bag, tapping each piece a little bit to remove any extra baking mix from

> 3- to 3 1/2-pound broiler-fryer chicken,
> cut into pieces

3. Arrange chicken pieces with the skin sides up and thickest parts to the outside edges in the dish.

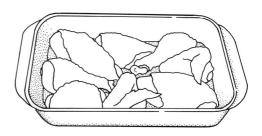

4. Cover with waxed paper, curled side down, and microwave on High (100%) 10 minutes. Turn the dish 1/2 turn.

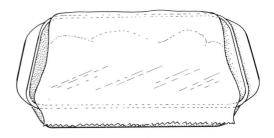

Cover with waxed paper, curled side down. When the handles are left uncovered, they won't get as warm.

5. Microwave 8 to 12 minutes longer or until the juices of the chicken run clear when cut with a sharp knife. Ask an adult to help. Using potholders, carefully remove the dish from the microwave. Carefully lift the edge of waxed paper farthest away from you to let the steam out, then remove the waxed paper.

HINTS: *Paprika is not always the same color—it can be bright red or dark red. The final color of the chicken will change with the paprika you use. Sprinkle on more paprika after cooking if you like.*

Quick Chicken Chunks

6 servings

INGREDIENTS

Whole boneless,
    skinless chicken
    breasts
Vegetable oil
Bisquick baking mix
Canned cornflake
    crumbs
Paprika
Salt
Pepper

UTENSILS

Cutting board
Sharp knife
Medium bowl
Fork
Measuring spoons
Dry measuring cups
Heavy plastic bag
    or shallow bowl
Microwavable dish
    with rack
Waxed paper

1. Ask an adult to help. Cut into 1-inch pieces

> 2 small whole boneless, skinless chicken breasts (about 1 pound)

2. Put the chicken pieces in the medium bowl and mix well with

> 1 tablespoon vegetable oil

Preceding page: Golden Chicken (page 86),
Cheesy Rice (page 114), Favorite Green Bean
Casserole (page 117)

3. Mix together in the plastic bag or shallow bowl

> 1/2 cup Bisquick baking mix
> 1/2 cup cornflake crumbs
> (from a can)
> 3/4 teaspoon paprika
> 1/4 teaspoon salt
> 1/4 teaspoon pepper

4. Shake about 6 chicken pieces at a time in the bag until coated. Shake off any extra crumbs.

5. Put the chicken pieces in a single layer on the rack in the dish.

6. Cover with waxed paper, curled side down, and microwave on High (100%) 3 minutes. Turn the dish 1/2 turn. Microwave 4 to 5 minutes longer or until juices run clear when chicken is cut with a sharp knife (ask an adult to help). Using potholders, carefully remove the dish from the microwave and lift the edge of waxed paper farthest away from you to let the steam out, then remove the waxed paper.

7. Serve with barbecue sauce if you like.

HINTS: *Serve these scrumptious "chunks" as a snack or for dinner. You may find using kitchen scissors makes cutting the chicken easier.*

For an easy honey-mustard sauce, mix equal amounts of honey and your favorite prepared mustard.

Mexican Chicken

4 servings

INGREDIENTS	UTENSILS
Bisquick baking mix	Heavy plastic bag
Yellow cornmeal	(1-gallon size)
Chili powder	Dry measuring cup
Paprika	Measuring spoons
Salt	Microwavable
Pepper	9-inch pie plate or
Chicken drumsticks,	8-inch square dish
thighs or wings	Waxed paper
	Potholders
	Sharp knife

1. Mix together in the plastic bag

> 1/2 cup Bisquick baking mix
> 2 tablespoons yellow cornmeal
> 2 teaspoons chili powder
> 1 teaspoon paprika
> 1/2 teaspoon salt
> 1/8 teaspoon pepper

2. Shake 2 pieces at a time in the bag until coated

> 8 chicken drumsticks, thighs or wings
> (about 2 pounds)

3. Arrange the chicken with the skin sides up and thickest parts to outside edge in the pie plate.

4. Cover with waxed paper, curled side down, and microwave on High (100%) 10 minutes. Turn the dish 1/2 turn. Re-cover and microwave 6 to 9 minutes longer or until juices run clear when the chicken is cut with a sharp knife (ask an adult to help). Using potholders, carefully remove the dish from the microwave. Carefully lift the edge of waxed paper farthest away from you to let the steam out, then remove the waxed paper.

HINTS: *Using all of the same kind of chicken pieces will help to cook the chicken evenly.*

*Mexican Chicken may become a favorite family dinner. **Sara** said, "It was fast and easy and the chicken was nice and moist."*

Italian Chicken and Spaghetti

6 servings

INGREDIENTS	UTENSILS
Broiler-fryer chicken, cut into pieces	Microwavable 3-quart casserole with lid
Onion	Potholders
Canned sliced mushrooms	Colander
Canned tomatoes	Container for fat
Canned tomato sauce	Cutting board
Sliced ripe olives	Sharp knife
Garlic powder	Medium bowl or 8-cup liquid measuring cup
Salt	Can opener
Dried oregano	Measuring spoons
Pepper	Dry measuring cup
Uncooked spaghetti	Long-handled spoon
Fresh parsley	Large saucepan

1. Arrange with skin sides up and thickest parts to outside edge in the casserole

> 3- to 3 1/2-pound broiler-fryer chicken, cut into pieces

2. Cover with the lid and microwave on High (100%) 12 minutes. (The chicken will be partially cooked.) Using potholders, carefully remove the casserole from the microwave. Remove the lid, lifting it from the side away from you, to let the steam out.

3. Put the colander over a container to hold any fat from the chicken. Ask an adult to pour the chicken carefully into the colander. Hot steam will rise so be careful. Put the chicken back into the casserole.

4. Peel, chop and put into the medium bowl

> 1 medium onion

5. Put the colander in the sink and pour in to drain

> 1 can (8 ounces) sliced mushrooms

6. Add the drained mushrooms and the following ingredients to the onion in the bowl and mix together well

> 1 can (16 ounces) tomatoes
> 1 can (8 ounces) tomato sauce
> 1/4 cup sliced ripe olives
> 1/2 teaspoon garlic powder
> 1 teaspoon salt
> 1 teaspoon dried oregano
> 1/4 teaspoon pepper

7. Stir the tomato mixture into the chicken in the casserole.

8. Cover with the lid and microwave on High (100%) 14 to 18 minutes or until juices of the chicken run clear when the chicken is cut with a sharp knife (ask an adult to help). Using potholders, carefully remove the casserole from the microwave. Remove the lid, lifting it from the side away from you, to let the steam out.

9. Ask an adult to cook on top of the stove, following the package directions

> 1 package (7 ounces) uncooked spaghetti

10. Put the colander in the sink. Ask an adult to carefully pour the spaghetti with the water into the colander. Hot steam will rise out of the sink, so be careful. Let the spaghetti stand a few minutes to drain well. Shake the colander several times to drain the water more quickly.

11. Serve the chicken over the spaghetti. Sprinkle with chopped parsley if you like.

HINT: *This recipe makes a large amount of food. Be sure to use the potholders and ask an adult to help.*

Mike *gave Italian Chicken and Spaghetti the best possible compliment. He said, "It was great. I loved putting all the stuff together. One of the best meals I have ever had." We like to hear that, Mike!*

FATHER'S DAY FESTIVITIES

Show your dad how much you love him by making this super-special meal for him.

> *Italian Chicken and Spaghetti (left)*
> *Tossed green salad*
> *Garlic Bread (page 119)*
> *Great Chocolate Cake (page 133)*

1. Make the Great Chocolate Cake
2. Make the Italian Chicken and Spaghetti
3. While the chicken is microwaving, prepare the Garlic Bread
4. Microwave the Garlic Bread right before serving it.

Mini Meatloaves

6 servings

INGREDIENTS

Milk
Egg
Hamburger meat
Fine dry bread
 crumbs
Ranch-style salad
 dressing mix (dry)
Worcestershire
 sauce

UTENSILS

Large bowl
Liquid measuring
 cup
Fork
Dry measuring cups
Long-handled
 spoon
Measuring spoons
Table knife
Microwavable dish
 with rack
Brush
Waxed paper
Potholders

1. Beat together with a fork in the large bowl

> 1/4 cup milk
> 1 egg

2. Mix into the egg mixture with a spoon or using your hands

> 1 pound hamburger meat
> 1/4 cup fine dry bread crumbs
> (from a can)
> 1 package (0.04 ounces) ranch-style
> salad dressing mix (dry)

3. Pat the meat mixture flat in the bottom of the bowl. Cut into 6 equal wedges.

4. Using your hands, shape each piece into a small loaf shaped like a football. Put the loaves in a circle or in rows on the rack in the dish.

5. Brush with

> 1 tablespoon Worcestershire sauce

6. Cover with waxed paper, curled side down. Microwave on High (100%) 5 minutes. Turn the dish 1/2 turn. Microwave 3 to 5 minutes longer or until the meat is no longer pink in the center (ask an adult to check by cutting with a knife). Using potholders, carefully remove the dish from the microwave. Carefully lift the edge of waxed paper farthest away from you to let the steam out.

7. Re-cover and let stand covered 5 minutes. Decorate with cheese strips, if desired.

Left: Mini Meatloaves, Colorful Corn (page 118)

Chiliburger Pie

6 to 8 servings

INGREDIENTS	UTENSILS
Lean hamburger meat or ground turkey	Medium bowl
	Long-handled spoon
Canned chili with beans	Microwavable 9-inch pie plate
Canned dry bread crumbs	Can opener
	Dry measuring cup
Instant chopped onion or onion, chopped	Measuring spoons
	Waxed paper
	Cutting board
Egg	Sharp knife
American cheese	Potholders
	Table knife

1. Mix together in the medium bowl

> 1 pound lean hamburger meat or
> ground turkey
> 1 can (7 1/2 ounces) chili with beans
> 1/2 cup fine dry bread crumbs
> (from a can)
> 1 tablespoon instant chopped onion
> or 1 small onion, chopped
> 1 egg

2. Press the meat mixture on the bottom and up the side of the pie plate.

3. Cover with waxed paper, curled side down, and microwave on High (100%) 5 minutes. Turn the pie plate 1/2 turn. Microwave 3 to 5 minutes longer or until the meat is no longer pink when you cut into the center with a knife (ask an adult to help). Using potholders, carefully remove the pie plate from the microwave. Carefully lift the edge of waxed paper farthest away from you to let the steam out, then remove the waxed paper.

4. Cut into 1-inch strips and arrange in a crisscross pattern over top

> 4 slices American cheese

5. Microwave uncovered on High (100%) about 1 minute or until the cheese is melted. Using potholders, remove the pie plate from the microwave.

6. Let stand uncovered 5 minutes before serving.

TACOBURGER PIE: Use 6 slices of American cheese to cover the top of the pie. After microwaving, top the pie with shredded lettuce, chopped tomatoes, sour cream and taco sauce.

HINTS: *If you like, put sliced olives, cherry tomato halves, sliced mushrooms or small crisscrossed pieces of sliced green bell pepper in the open squares after microwaving.*

This recipe calls for lean hamburger meat so you don't have to drain off juices. If some juices do form, have an adult help you remove the liquid with a spoon.

Spaghetti Pizza Pie

6 servings

INGREDIENTS	UTENSILS
Uncooked spaghetti	Large saucepan
Margarine or butter	Colander
Dried oregano	Potholders
leaves	Large bowl
Grated Parmesan	Measuring spoons
cheese	Fork
Shredded	Table knife
mozzarella cheese	Long-handled
Canned tomato	spoon
sauce	Rubber scraper
Canned sliced	Dry measuring cups
mushrooms	Microwavable
Thin-sliced	9-inch pie plate
pepperoni	Can opener

1. Ask an adult to cook on top of the stove in the large saucepan, following the package directions—except break in half before putting into the water (it's easier to mix later on)

> 1 package (7 ounces) uncooked spaghetti

2. Put the colander in the sink. Ask an adult to pour the spaghetti with the water carefully into the colander. Hot steam will rise, so be careful. Let the spaghetti stand a few minutes to drain well. Shake the colander several times to drain the water more quickly.

3. Pour the spaghetti into the bowl. Stir in until the margarine is melted

> 1 tablespoon margarine or butter
> 1 teaspoon dried oregano leaves

4. Stir in

> 1/3 cup grated Parmesan cheese
> 1 cup shredded mozzarella cheese
> (4 ounces)

5. Pour the spaghetti mixture into the pie plate. Using the back of a large spoon, press evenly onto the bottom and up the side of the pie plate.

6. Microwave uncovered on High (100%) 2 minutes. Turn the pie plate 1/2 turn. Microwave 1 to 2 minutes longer or until the cheese is melted and the crust is firm.

7. Ask an adult to help. Using potholders, carefully remove the pie from the microwave.

Preceding page: Spaghetti Pizza Pie (page 96), Chiliburger Pie (page 94)

8. Spoon onto and spread evenly over the spaghetti

> 1 can (8 ounces) tomato sauce

9. Put the strainer in the sink and pour in to drain

> 1 can (4 ounces) sliced mushrooms

10. Arrange the drained mushrooms evenly over the tomato sauce along with

> 1/2 package (3 1/2 ounces) thin-sliced pepperoni
> 1 cup shredded mozzarella cheese (4 ounces)

11. Microwave uncovered on High (100%) 2 minutes. Turn the pie plate 1/2 turn. Microwave 2 to 3 minutes longer until the cheese is melted and the center of the pie is hot. Ask an adult to help. Using potholders, remove the pie plate from the microwave.

12. Let stand uncovered about 5 minutes before serving.

HINT: *If you like bell pepper, add 1/4 cup chopped green bell pepper along with the mushrooms.*

Erin *commented, "We put 8 ounces of cheese with the spaghetti and 4 ounces on top. It's delicious! I always thought mushrooms were gross, but this recipe made them taste great! I will definitely make it again." Maybe you'll rethink mushrooms, too.*

 # Easy Spaghetti

4 servings

INGREDIENTS

Uncooked spaghetti
Hamburger meat
Chunky spaghetti
  sauce
Grated Parmesan
  cheese

UTENSILS

Large saucepan
Microwavable
  1 1/2-quart
  casserole
Waxed paper
Long-handled
  spoon
Colander
Container for fat
Potholders

1. Ask an adult to help. Cook on top of the stove in the saucepan, following the package directions

1 package (7 ounces) uncooked spaghetti

2. While the spaghetti is cooking, with your fingers crumble into small pieces into the casserole

1/2 pound hamburger meat

3. Cover with waxed paper, curled side down, and microwave on High (100%) 2 minutes. Stir to break up the meat.

4. Re-cover and microwave on High (100%) 2 to 3 minutes longer or until the meat is no longer pink. Carefully remove the waxed paper. To avoid steam, lift the corner farthest away from you first.

5. Put the colander over the container to hold any fat from the meat. Ask an adult to pour the meat carefully into the colander. Hot steam will rise so be careful.

6. Put the meat back into the casserole. Stir in

1 jar (16 ounces) chunky spaghetti sauce

7. Cover with waxed paper, curled side down, and microwave on High (100%) 3 to 4 minutes or until hot. Using potholders, carefully remove the casserole from the microwave and lift the edge of waxed paper farthest away from you to let the steam out, then remove the waxed paper.

8. Put the colander in the sink. Ask an adult to pour the spaghetti with the water carefully into the colander. Again, hot steam will rise out of the sink, so be careful. Let the spaghetti stand a few minutes to drain well. Shake the colander several times to drain the water more quickly.

9. Serve the sauce over the cooked spaghetti and sprinkle with

1/4 cup grated Parmesan cheese

Cowabunga Casserole

6 servings

INGREDIENTS

Super Good Taco Salad meat mixture (page 114)

Spiral macaroni (rotini)

Frozen mixed vegetables

Canned tomato or spaghetti sauce

UTENSILS

3-quart saucepan
Colander
Potholders
Microwavable 2-quart casserole with lid
Spoon
Fork
Dry measuring cups
Can opener
Rubber scraper

1. Prepare the Super Good Taco Salad meat mixture as directed, but stop *after* Step 6 when the meat is cooked.

2. Ask an adult to cook on top of the stove in the saucepan, following the package directions

> 1 package (5 ounces) spiral macaroni (rotini)

3. Put the colander in the sink. Ask an adult to pour carefully the macaroni with the water into the colander. Hot steam will rise out of the sink, so be careful. Let the macaroni stand a few minutes to drain well. Shake the colander several times to drain the water more quickly.

4. Unwrap and put into the casserole

> 1 package (10 ounces) frozen mixed vegetables

5. Cover with the lid and microwave on High (100%) 5 minutes. Stir.

6. Stir in the cooked macaroni until evenly mixed along with

> 2 cups Super Good Taco Salad meat mixture
> 1 can (15 ounces) tomato or spaghetti sauce

7. Cover with the lid and microwave on High (100%) 5 minutes. Stir. Re-cover and microwave 5 to 7 minutes longer or until hot. Using potholders, carefully remove the casserole from the microwave. Remove the lid, lifting it from the side away from you, to let the steam out.

Lazy Lasagne

6 servings

INGREDIENTS	UTENSILS
Easy Spaghetti sauce (page 98)	1 1/2-quart microwavable casserole or bowl
Instant lasagne noodles	Waxed paper
Small curd cottage cheese	Potholders
	Colander
Grated Parmesan cheese	Container for fat
	2 spoons
Egg	Dry measuring cups
Shredded mozzarella cheese (4 ounces)	Microwavable 8-inch square dish
	Small bowl

1. Prepare the sauce for Easy Spaghetti (page 98) as directed but stop *after* Step 6 when the spaghetti sauce is stirred into the meat. Do not prepare the spaghetti.

2. Spread 1 cup of the meat sauce in the bottom of the square dish.

3. Rinse quickly under running water, then put next to each other, and overlapping a little bit, on top of sauce

> 3 instant lasagne noodles

4. Mix together in the small bowl and spread over the noodles

> 1 cup small curd cottage cheese
> 1/4 cup grated Parmesan cheese
> 1 egg

5. Spoon about 2/3 cup of the meat sauce over the cheese mixture. The cheese mixture will not be completely covered.

6. Rinse 3 more lasagne noodles under running water. Put on top of the sauce, overlapping a little.

7. Spoon the rest of the meat sauce over the noodles. Cover the dish with waxed paper, curled side down, and microwave on High (100%) 8 minutes.

8. Ask an adult to help. Turn the dish 1/2 turn. Microwave on High (100%) 8 to 10 minutes longer or until the lasagne is hot and bubbly.

9. Ask an adult to help. Using potholders, carefully remove the dish from the microwave. Lift the edge of the waxed paper farthest away from you to let the steam out, then remove the waxed paper.

10. Immediately sprinkle with

> 1 cup shredded mozzarella cheese
> (4 ounces)

11. Let the lasagne stand uncovered 10 minutes or until the cheese is melted before serving.

Cheddar Scalloped Potatoes

8 servings

INGREDIENTS	UTENSILS
Canned condensed cream of chicken soup or cream of mushroom soup	Microwavable 2-quart casserole with lid
Milk	Rubber scraper
Potatoes	Liquid measuring cup
Instant chopped onion	Cutting board
	Sharp knife
Shredded Cheddar cheese	Dry measuring cups
Salt	Measuring spoons
Pepper	Long-handled spoon
Parmesan cheese, if you like	Potholders
	Fork

1. Pour into the casserole

> 1 can (10 3/4 ounces) condensed cream of chicken or cream of mushroom soup

2. While stirring, add a little at a time, until all the milk is added

> 3/4 cup milk

3. Scrub and cut into 1/8-inch slices (to measure 4 cups)

> About 4 medium potatoes

4. Stir the potato slices into the mixture in the casserole along with

> 1 tablespoon instant chopped onion or 1 small onion, chopped

5. Add, stirring until well mixed,

> 1 cup shredded Cheddar cheese (4 ounces)
> 1/2 teaspoon salt
> 1/8 teaspoon pepper

6. Cover with the lid and microwave on High (100%) 10 minutes. Using potholders, carefully remove the lid, lifting from the side away from you, to let the steam out. Stir. Re-cover and microwave 10 to 15 minutes longer or until the potatoes are tender when poked with a fork. Using potholders, remove the casserole from the microwave. Carefully remove the lid, lifting from the side away from you, to let the steam out.

7. Stir. Sprinkle with Parmesan cheese.

Sara *said, "Instead of cream of chicken soup, I used cream of mushroom soup. It was really, really good!" We liked Sara's idea so much that we added cream of mushroom soup.*

Cheesy Macaroni

4 servings

INGREDIENTS	UTENSILS
Elbow macaroni	3-quart saucepan
Process American cheese	Long-handled spoon
Margarine or butter	Colander
Milk	Microwavable 2-quart casserole with lid
	Potholders
	Cutting board
	Sharp knife
	Table knife
	Measuring spoons
	Liquid measuring cup

1. Ask an adult to cook on top of the stove in the saucepan, following the package directions

> 1 package (7 ounces) elbow macaroni (about 1 3/4 cups)

2. Put the colander in the sink. Ask an adult to carefully pour the macaroni with the water into the colander. Hot steam will rise so be careful. Let the macaroni stand a few minutes to drain well. Shake the colander several times to drain the water more quickly.

3. Cut into cubes and put into the casserole

> 8 ounces process American cheese (about 1 1/2 cups 1/2-inch cubes)

4. Add to the cheese

> 2 tablespoons margarine or butter
> 2/3 cup milk

5. Cover with the lid and microwave on High (100%) 3 minutes. Stir. Re-cover and microwave about 2 minutes or until the sauce is smooth when stirred. Using potholders, carefully remove the casserole from the microwave. Carefully remove the lid, lifting it from the side away from you to let the steam out.

6. Carefully stir the cooked macaroni, a little at a time, into the cheese sauce until all the macaroni is added and it's evenly mixed.

7. Cover with the lid and microwave on High (100%) 3 to 4 minutes or until hot. Using potholders, carefully remove the casserole from the microwave. Remember to be careful when you remove the lid.

HINTS: *For something different, stir one of the following into the cheese sauce: 1/4 cup sliced or chopped olives, green onion or bell pepper, or 1/2 cup chopped cooked smoked ham. A wire whisk works best to stir the sauce smooth.*

Macaroni and cheese is an American favorite. **Betsy** *explains why so many people love it: "I like the taste and it was easy to make."*

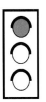

Hot Dogs and Cheese Potatoes

4 servings

INGREDIENTS	UTENSILS
Microwaved Potatoes (page 13)	Sharp knife
	Cutting board
	Spoon
Hot dogs	Microwavable 4-cup glass measuring cup
Pasteurized process cheese spread (plain or Mexican)	
	Measuring spoons
Milk	Waxed paper
Chopped parsley	Potholders

1. Microwave as directed and save

> 4 Microwaved Potatoes

2. Cut crosswise into chunks about 1/2 inch wide and save

> 4 hot dogs

3. Spoon into the glass measuring cup

> 1 jar (8 ounces) pasteurized process cheese spread (plain or Mexican)

4. Add

> 2 tablespoons milk

5. Cover with waxed paper, curled side down. Microwave on High (100%) 1 minute.

6. Remove the measuring cup from the microwave. Carefully remove the waxed paper to avoid steam by lifting a corner farthest away from you first. Stir in the hot dog pieces.

7. Re-cover and microwave on High (100%) 1 to 2 minutes longer or until hot.

8. Cut a slit the long way in the top of each potato. Using potholders, carefully push each side of the potato toward the center so the potato opens up. Be careful of the steam.

9. Stir the cheese mixture and pour over the potatoes.

10. Sprinkle *each* potato with

> 1/2 teaspoon chopped parsley

HINT: *This main dish is easy to make with leftover chopped, cooked meat such as ham, turkey or beef instead of the hot dogs. You can add leftover cooked vegetables that you've chopped up, too.*

Really Good Ravioli

6 servings

INGREDIENTS

Hamburger meat or
  ground turkey
Onion
Canned ravioli
Shredded
  mozzarella cheese

UTENSILS

Microwavable
  2-quart casserole
  with lid
Cutting board
Sharp knife
Potholders
Long-handled
  spoon
Colander
Container for fat
Can opener

1. With your fingers, crumble into small pieces into the casserole

> 1 pound hamburger meat or ground turkey

2. Peel, chop and add to the meat

> 1 small onion

3. Cover with the lid and microwave on High (100%) 3 minutes. Stir. Re-cover and microwave 2 to 3 minutes longer or until the meat is no longer pink. Using potholders, carefully remove the casserole from the microwave. Remove the lid, lifting it from the side away from you, to let the steam out.

4. Put the colander over a container to hold any fat from the meat. Ask an adult to pour the meat carefully into the colander. Hot steam will rise so be careful. Put the meat back into the casserole.

5. Stir in

> 2 cans (15 ounces each) ravioli

6. Cover with the lid and microwave on High (100%) 3 minutes. Remember to be careful when you remove the lid. Stir. Re-cover and microwave 2 to 4 minutes longer or until hot. Using potholders, re-move the casserole from the microwave.

7. Sprinkle with

> 1 cup shredded mozzarella cheese (4 ounces)

8. Re-cover and let stand until the cheese is melted.

HINT: *It's fun to use different flavors of cheese on top of this casserole. Try Cheddar cheese or pizza- or taco-flavored cheese for variety.*

Really Good Ravioli

Crunchy Pasta and Cheese

2 servings

INGREDIENTS

Canned pasta in
  tomato and cheese
  sauce
Corn chips
Shredded American
  cheese

UTENSILS

Can opener
Microwavable
  1-quart casserole
  with lid
Potholders
Large spoon
Dry measuring cups

1. Pour into the casserole

> 1 can (15 ounces) pasta in tomato and
> cheese sauce

2. Cover with the lid and microwave on High (100%) 3 minutes. Using potholders, carefully remove the lid, lifting from the side away from you, to let the steam out. Stir.

3. Sprinkle with

> 1 package (1.5 ounces) corn chips

4. Sprinkle over the chips

> 1/4 cup shredded American cheese
> (1 ounce)

5. Microwave uncovered on High (100%) 30 to 60 seconds or until the cheese is melted. Using potholders, carefully remove the casserole from the microwave.

*Crunchy Pasta and Cheese was a big hit in **Erin's** family. She told us, "It's fun, quick and easy to make. Even my fussy five-year-old brother liked it. Adding chips and cheese to this pasta made it taste tons better than eating it plain out of the can."*

Turkey Lurkey Chili

6 servings

INGREDIENTS

Ground turkey,
  hamburger meat
  or ground pork
Celery
Onion
Canned pinto
  beans
Chili powder
Canned stewed
  tomatoes
Canned tomato
  sauce
Shredded cheese
Sliced ripe olives

UTENSILS

Microwavable
  2-quart casserole
  with lid
Cutting board
Sharp knife
Spoon
Colander
Container for fat
Potholders
Can opener
Measuring spoons

1. With your fingers, crumble into small pieces into the casserole

> 1 pound ground turkey, hamburger meat or ground pork

2. Wash the celery, peel the onion, chop and add to the turkey

> 1 stalk celery
> 1 small onion

3. Cover with the lid and microwave on High (100%) 2 minutes. Stir. Re-cover and microwave 2 to 3 minutes longer or until the turkey is no longer pink. Using potholders, carefully remove the casserole from the microwave. Carefully remove the lid, lifting it from the side away from you, to let the steam out.

4. Put the colander over a container to hold any fat from the turkey. Ask an adult to help. Using potholders, carefully pour the turkey into the colander. Hot steam will rise so be careful. Put the turkey back into the casserole.

5. Pour into the colander to drain

> 1 can (15 1/2 ounces) pinto beans

6. Add the pinto beans to the casserole and stir in

> 1 tablespoon chili powder
> 1 can (14 1/2 ounces) stewed tomatoes, undrained
> 1 can (8 ounces) tomato sauce

7. Cover with the lid and microwave on High (100%) 5 minutes. Stir. Re-cover and microwave 3 to 5 minutes longer or until hot. Using potholders, carefully remove the casserole from the microwave.

8. Let stand covered 5 minutes for the flavors to blend.

9. Serve with

> Shredded cheese
> Sliced ripe olives

Seaside Casserole

6 servings

INGREDIENTS

Carrot
Celery
Canned tuna in
  water
Instant rice
Canned cream-style
  corn
Milk
Cheese-flavored
  fish-shaped
  crackers

UTENSILS

Vegetable peeler
Cutting board
Sharp knife
Shredder
Can opener
Large strainer
Dry measuring cups
Long-handled
  spoon
Liquid measuring
  cup
Microwavable
  2-quart casserole
  with lid
Potholders
Spoon

1. Wash, peel and shred

> 1 medium carrot

2. Wash and chop

> 1 medium stalk celery

3. Put the strainer in the sink and put in to drain

> 2 cans (6 1/2 ounces each) tuna in water

4. Mix the carrot, celery and tuna together in the casserole. Stir in

> 1 cup instant rice
> 1 can (16 ounces) cream-style corn
> 1/2 cup milk

5. Cover with the lid and microwave on High (100%) 5 minutes. Stir. Re-cover and microwave 4 to 6 minutes longer or until the rice is no longer hard. Using potholders, carefully remove the casserole from the microwave. Carefully remove the lid, lifting from the side away from you, to let the steam out.

6. Stir the casserole and sprinkle with

> 1 cup cheese-flavored fish-shaped crackers

BARNYARD CASSEROLE: Use 2 cans (5 ounces each) chunk chicken in place of tuna, and tiny duck-shaped crackers instead of fish-shaped crackers.

HINT: *Crackers can become soggy if they are microwaved with the casserole. That's why it's best to sprinkle them on top at the end.*

Seaside Casserole

Shoestring and Cheese Pie

6 servings

INGREDIENTS

Frozen uncooked
deep-dish 9-inch
pie crust
Worcestershire
sauce
Shredded Cheddar
cheese
Bacon flavor bits
Eggs
Canned evaporated
milk
Canned shoestring
potatoes
Dried chives or
parsley flakes

UTENSILS

Microwavable
9-inch pie plate
Fork
Pastry brush
Potholders
Measuring spoons
Dry measuring cups
Medium bowl
Eggbeater
Can opener
Microwavable
dinner plate
Waxed paper

1. Have an adult help you carefully take out of the aluminum foil pie pan and put into the pie plate

> 1 frozen uncooked deep-dish 9-inch pie crust (1/2 of 12-ounce package)

2. Microwave the pie crust uncovered on High (100%) 1 minute or until thawed (not cooked).

3. Poke the bottom and sides of the crust with a fork so it won't puff up. Brush the pie crust with

> 1 teaspoon Worcestershire sauce

4. Microwave uncovered on High (100%) 2 minutes. Using potholders, carefully turn the dish 1/2 turn. Microwave about 2 minutes longer or until the crust looks dry. Using potholders, carefully remove from the microwave.

5. Sprinkle the bottom of the pie shell evenly with

> 1 cup shredded Cheddar cheese (4 ounces)
> 2 tablespoons bacon flavor bits

6. Beat with eggbeater in the medium bowl until mixed, and pour over the cheese

> 3 eggs
> 1 can (5 ounces) evaporated milk

7. Sprinkle evenly over the top

> 1 can (1 3/4 ounces) shoestring potatoes
> 1 tablespoon dried chives or parsley flakes

8. Put the dinner plate upside down in the microwave. Ask an adult to help you put the pie on top of the dinner plate. Put a piece of waxed paper, curled side down, on top of the pie.

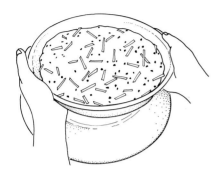

9. Microwave uncovered on Medium (50%) 6 minutes. Using potholders, turn the pie plate 1/2 turn. Microwave 5 to 7 minutes longer or until a knife stuck into the pie 1 inch from the middle comes out clean (center should be almost set).

10. Using potholders, ask an adult to remove the pie from the microwave and put it on a flat, heatproof surface (not a wire rack). Let it stand uncovered 10 minutes.

HINTS: *Pie plates without handles can get hotter than other types of dishes so ask an adult to help, and always use potholders when handling hot pie plates. If the microwave won't be used right after cooking the pie, open the door and let the pie stand uncovered for the 10 minutes.*

If the pie crust cracks a little after it is thawed (just before poking it with a fork), press the crust together with your fingers. Brush Worcestershire sauce on the top edge of the crust again before microwaving to make it a little brown. Leftover ham or crumbled cooked bacon can be used in place of the bacon bits if you like.

DINNER FOR MOM

Mom will love these treats on Mother's Day, her birthday or *any* day.

Shoestring and Cheese Pie (left)
Sliced tomatoes with dressing
Berry Muffins (page 79)
Puffy Pebble Pie (page 129)

1. Make the Puffy Pebble Pie first (or a day ahead).
2. Make the Berry Muffins next.
3. Make the Shoestring and Cheese Pie.

Chunky Chowder

4 to 6 servings (about 1 1/4 cups each)

INGREDIENTS

Tiny cooked, smoked sausage links or regular-size links
Canned condensed cream of potato soup
Canned vacuum-packed whole kernel corn with red and green peppers
Canned cream-style corn
Instant chopped onion or fresh onion, chopped
Milk

UTENSILS

Microwavable 2-quart casserole with lid
Spoon
Potholders
Cutting board
Sharp knife
Can opener
Rubber scraper
Measuring spoons
Liquid measuring cup

1. Put into the casserole

> 1/2 pound tiny fully cooked, smoked sausage links or regular-size links, cut into 1/2-inch chunks

2. Stir together in the casserole until evenly mixed

> 1 can (10 3/4 ounces) condensed cream of potato soup
> 1 can (11 ounces) vacuum-packed whole kernel corn with red and green peppers
> 1 can (8 ounces) cream-style corn
> 1 tablespoon instant chopped onion or 1 small onion, chopped
> 1 cup milk

3. Cover with the lid and microwave on High (100%) 6 minutes. Stir. Re-cover and microwave 3 to 5 minutes longer or until hot.

4. Ask an adult to help. Using potholders, remove the casserole from the microwave.

HINT: *We really liked the tiny smoked sausages in this recipe instead of the regular-size links. You only need half of a 1-pound package.*

Chunky Chowder

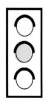

Cheesy Rice

6 servings

INGREDIENTS

Instant rice
Water
Margarine or butter
Shredded
  mozzarella or
  American cheese

UTENSILS

Microwavable
  3-quart casserole
  with lid
Liquid measuring
  cup
Long-handled
  spoon
Table knife
Dry measuring cups
Measuring spoons
Potholders

1. Put into the casserole

> 2 cups instant rice
> 1 1/2 cups water
> 2 tablespoons margarine or butter

2. Cover with the lid and microwave on High (100%) 7 to 9 minutes or until the rice is tender and the water is absorbed. Using potholders, carefully remove the casserole from the microwave and remove the lid, lifting from the side away from you, to let the steam out.

3. Stir in

> 3/4 cup shredded mozzarella or
> American cheese (3 ounces)

4. Serve right away while the cheese is still stringy. If you like, sprinkle some chopped parsley over the rice.

Super Good Taco Salad

4 servings

INGREDIENTS

Hamburger meat
Instant chopped
  onion or fresh
  onion, chopped
Canned kidney
  beans
Taco seasoning mix
Water
Canned tomato
  sauce
Tomatoes
Lettuce
Regular-size corn
  chips
Shredded Cheddar
  cheese
Sour cream

UTENSILS

Microwavable
  2-quart casserole
  with lid
Cutting board
Sharp knife
Potholders
Spoon
Colander
Container for fat
Can opener
Liquid measuring
  cup
Rubber scraper
Dry measuring cups
4 dinner plates

1. With your fingers, crumble into small pieces into the casserole

> 1 1/2 pounds hamburger meat

2. Sprinkle over the meat

> 1 tablespoon instant chopped onion or 1 small onion, chopped

3. Cover with the lid and microwave on High (100%) 4 minutes. Stir. Re-cover and microwave 4 to 5 minutes longer or until the meat is no longer pink. Using potholders, carefully remove the casserole from the microwave. Carefully remove the lid, lifting from the side away from you, to let the steam out.

4. Put the colander over the container to hold any fat from the meat. Ask an adult to pour the meat mixture carefully into the colander. Hot steam will rise so be careful. Put the meat back into the casserole. Pour into the colander

> 1 can (16 ounces) kidney beans

5. Stir the drained kidney beans into the beef mixture along with

> 1 package (1 1/4 ounces) taco seasoning mix
> 1/4 cup water
> 1 can (8 ounces) tomato sauce

6. Cover with the lid and microwave on High (100%) 3 minutes. Stir. Re-cover and microwave 3 to 4 minutes until hot. Using potholders, remove the casserole from the microwave.

7. Wash and chop

> 2 medium tomatoes

8. Layer 1 cup of each on *each* of the plates

> 4 cups small pieces lettuce (about 1/2 medium head)
> 4 cups regular-size corn chips

9. Top *each* serving with about 1/3 cup of the chopped tomatoes.

10. Measure out 2 cups of the meat mixture. Cover it and refrigerate or freeze. Divide and spoon the rest of the meat mixture over the tomatoes. Top *each* serving with about

> 2 tablespoons shredded Cheddar cheese
> 1 tablespoon sour cream

HINT: *The 2 cups of meat mixture that's left over is the perfect amount for the Cowabunga Casserole (page 99).*

Favorite Green Bean Casserole

6 servings

INGREDIENTS	UTENSILS
Canned condensed cream of celery, cream of chicken or cream of mushroom soup	Microwavable 2-quart casserole with lid
Milk	Can opener
Diced pimientos	Long-handled spoon
Pepper	Liquid measuring cup
Canned cut green beans	Measuring spoons
Canned French fried onions	Strainer
	Potholders

1. Mix together in the casserole

> 1 can (10 3/4 ounces) condensed cream of celery, cream of chicken or cream of mushroom soup
> 1/4 cup milk
> 1 jar (2 ounces) diced pimientos, undrained
> 1/8 teaspoon pepper

Super Good Taco Salad (page 114), Corn-and-Bacon Muffins (page 120)

2. Put the strainer in the sink and pour in to drain

> 2 cans (16 ounces each) cut green beans

3. Stir the beans into the soup mixture. Cover with the lid and microwave on High (100%) 5 minutes. Using potholders, carefully remove the lid, lifting from the side away from you, to let the steam out.

4. Stir. Sprinkle the top with

> 1 can (2.8 ounces) French fried onions

5. Microwave uncovered on High (100%) 3 to 5 minutes or until hot. Using potholders, carefully remove the casserole from the microwave.

HINT: *The canned green beans make this recipe faster than ever. If frozen green beans are used, use a 16-ounce package and follow the directions for microwaving on the package, cooking the minimum time and draining before mixing with the soup mixture.*

Colorful Corn

4 servings

INGREDIENTS	UTENSILS
Sliced pimientos	Small strainer
Frozen whole kernel corn	Microwavable 1-quart casserole with lid
Margarine or butter	Table knife
Dried basil leaves	Measuring spoons
Salt	Cutting board
Green onions	Sharp knife
Shredded Monterey Jack or Cheddar cheese	Dry measuring cups
	Spoon
	Potholders

1. Put the strainer in the sink and put in to drain

> 1 jar (2 ounces) sliced pimientos

2. Mix together in the casserole the drained pimientos and

> 1 package (10 ounces) frozen whole kernel corn
> 1 tablespoon margarine or butter
> 1/4 teaspoon dried basil leaves
> 1/4 teaspoon salt

3. Cover with the lid and microwave on High (100%) according to the time on the package of corn.

4. Wash and chop

> 2 green onions (with tops)

5. Using potholders, carefully remove the lid, lifting from the side away from you, to let the steam out. Stir in onions along with

> 1/2 cup shredded Monterey Jack or Cheddar cheese (2 ounces)

6. Cover with the lid and microwave on High (100%) 1 minute or until the cheese just begins to melt.

7. Let stand covered about 1 minute before serving. Using potholders, carefully remove the casserole from the microwave. Remove the lid, lifting from the side away from you, to let the steam out.

Garlic Bread

About 10 slices

INGREDIENTS

French or Italian
bread
Margarine or butter
Garlic powder or
chopped garlic

UTENSILS

Cutting board
Sharp serrated
knife
Microwavable
9-inch pie plate
Measuring spoons
Dry measuring cups
Waxed paper
Fork
Microwavable
paper towels or
napkins
Microwavable
dinner plate

1. Cut into 1-inch slices

1/2 loaf (1-pound size) French or
Italian bread

2. Put into the pie plate

1/2 cup margarine or butter
1/4 to 1/2 teaspoon garlic powder
or chopped garlic

3. Cover with waxed paper, curled side down, and microwave on High (100%) 45 to 60 seconds or until the margarine is melted. Stir with a fork to mix in garlic evenly.

4. Dip 1 cut side of each bread slice into the margarine and put the loaf back together.

5. Put a paper towel or napkin on the dinner plate. Put half the bread on 1 side of the plate and put the other half of the bread next to it.

6. Cover with a paper towel and microwave on Medium (50%) 30 seconds. Turn the plate 1/2 turn. Microwave on Medium (50%) 30 to 45 seconds longer or until the bread is warm.

CHEESE-GARLIC BREAD: After putting the bread together on the plate, put 1 thin slice of cheese between each of the bread slices. Add 30 seconds to each cooking time, microwaving until the cheese is slightly melted.

HINT: *If you like, sprinkle the bread slices with chopped chives after dipping in the margarine.*

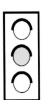

Corn-and-Bacon Muffins

6 servings

INGREDIENTS

Bacon
Grated Parmesan
  cheese
Paprika
Margarine or butter
Milk
Egg
Golden corn muffin
  mix

UTENSILS

2 microwavable
  paper towels
Microwavable
  dinner plate
Small bowl
Measuring spoons
Table knife
Liquid measuring
  cup
6 paper baking
  cups
Microwavable
  muffin ring
Medium bowl
Spoon
Dry measuring cups
Rubber scraper
Toothpick
Potholders

1. Put a paper towel on the microwavable plate. Put side by side on the towel

2 slices bacon

2. Put the other paper towel on top of the bacon. Microwave on High (100%) 1 1/2 to 2 1/2 minutes or until the bacon is brown. Carefully take the paper towel off the top of the bacon and let stand about 5 minutes.

3. Break the bacon into small pieces. Save.

4. Mix in the small bowl and save

1 tablespoon grated Parmesan cheese 1/4 teaspoon paprika

5. Put 1 paper baking cup into each cup of the muffin ring.

6. Put in the medium bowl

2 tablespoons margarine or butter

7. Microwave uncovered on High (100%) 15 to 30 seconds or until melted. Add to the bowl and beat in

1/4 cup milk 1 egg

8. Stir in just until all the mix is wet (the batter will be lumpy)

1 pouch (6.25 ounces) golden corn muffin mix

9. Carefully stir in the bacon pieces.

10. Fill each cup with about 1/4 cup batter. Sprinkle with 1/2 teaspoon Parmesan cheese mixture.

11. Microwave uncovered on High (100%) 1 minute. Turn the muffin ring 1/4 turn.

12. Microwave on High (100%) 1 to 2 minutes longer, turning 1/4 turn every minute, until a toothpick poked in the centers comes out clean. Using potholders, carefully remove the muffin ring from the microwave.

13. Let the muffins stand in the ring uncovered about 5 minutes to cool slightly. Carefully remove the muffins from the ring. Serve warm.

If you don't have a microwave muffin ring, you can still make microwave muffins. Use 6 paper hot drink cups. Using kitchen scissors, cut off the top of the cup so there's only 1 inch left on the bottom. Arrange the 6 "short" cups in a circle on a microwave dinner plate and line with paper baking cups. Prepare the recipe as directed. Save the cups to use again.

HINTS: *An easy way to fill the muffin cups is to use an ice-cream scoop with a spring handle. Scoops come in different sizes and the right size to use is a No. 24. When you're cooking the muffins, it's easier to keep track of the turns by putting a little piece of tape on the muffin ring. Always turn the muffin ring in the same direction. If you don't have a microwavable muffin ring, see the special tip at the left. This tip can also be used for Berry Muffins, page 79.*

CHAPTER

5

ANYTIME
SWEETS
AND
DESSERTS

Pineapple Puddle Cakes (page 134), Fudgy Peppermint Sauce (page 128), Great Chocolate Cake (page 133)

Awesome Apple Crisp

2 servings

INGREDIENTS

Tart cooking apples
Quick-cooking oats
  (not instant)
All-purpose flour
Packed brown
  sugar
Margarine or
  butter, softened
Ground cinnamon

UTENSILS

Vegetable peeler
Cutting board
Sharp knife
2 microwavable
  10-ounce custard
  cups
Measuring spoons
Small bowl
Table knife or metal
  spatula
Fork
Potholders

1. Peel and slice

> 2 medium tart cooking apples

2. Divide the apple slices between the custard cups.

3. Make a topping by mixing in the small bowl, then sprinkling over the apples

> 2 tablespoons quick-cooking oats
>   (not instant)
> 2 tablespoons all-purpose flour
> 2 tablespoons packed brown sugar
> 2 tablespoons margarine or butter,
>   softened
> 1/4 teaspoon ground cinnamon

4. Microwave uncovered on High (100%) 5 to 6 minutes or until the apples are tender when poked with a fork. Using potholders, remove the cups from the microwave.

5. Let the apples stand uncovered 10 minutes.

BUTTERSCOTCH APPLE CRISP: Stir 1 tablespoon butterscotch-flavored chips into the crumbly mixture.

HINT: *Put the custard cups on a microwavable dinner plate to make them easier to handle.*

Chocolate-Cherry Cobbler

6 servings

INGREDIENTS

Canned cherry pie
  filling
Margarine or butter
Semisweet
  chocolate chips
All-purpose flour
Sugar
Chopped nuts
Vanilla
Egg
Whipped topping
  or ice cream, if
  you like.

UTENSILS

Microwavable
  8-inch round dish
Can opener
Rubber scraper
Microwavable
  4-cup glass
  measuring cup
Table knife or metal
  spatula
Dry measuring cups
Measuring spoons
Long-handled
  spoon
Cutting board
Sharp knife
Potholders

1. Pour into the round dish and spread evenly

> 1 can (21 ounces) cherry pie filling

2. Microwave the pie filling uncovered on High (100%) 3 minutes. Stir.

3. Put in the glass measuring cup

> 1/4 cup margarine or butter
> 1/2 cup semisweet chocolate chips

4. Microwave uncovered on High (100%) 30 to 60 seconds or until the mixture can be stirred smooth. Cool a few minutes.

5. Mix into the chocolate mixture until smooth (batter will be stiff)

> 3/4 cup all-purpose flour
> 1/2 cup sugar
> 1/3 cup chopped nuts
> 1 teaspoon vanilla
> 1 egg

6. Drop 8 spoonfuls of batter in a circle around the outside edge of the round dish. Don't put any dough in the center of the dish. Microwave uncovered on High (100%) 3 minutes. Turn the dish 1/4 turn.

7. Microwave uncovered on High (100%) 3 minutes. Turn the dish 1/4 turn. Microwave 3 to 6 minutes longer or until the batter looks dry. Using potholders, remove from the microwave.

8. Let stand uncovered on a flat, heatproof surface (not on a wire rack) at least 30 minutes. This dessert is very hot—be sure to wait long enough.

9. Serve with whipped topping or ice cream.

HINT: *Putting the dough in a circle helps the cobbler to cook evenly.*

Triple Chocolate Pudding

4 servings

INGREDIENTS

Chocolate milk
Milk chocolate or
 chocolate pudding
 and pie filling (not
 instant)
Milk chocolate bars
Whipped topping
 or whipped cream

UTENSILS

Microwavable
 4-cup glass
 measuring cup
Wire whisk
Rubber scraper
Potholders
4 serving dishes
Spoon
Plastic wrap

1. Measure into the glass measuring cup

> 2 cups chocolate milk

2. Stir in with the wire whisk until dissolved

> 1 package (3 1/2 ounces) milk
> chocolate or chocolate pudding and
> pie filling (not instant)

3. Microwave uncovered on High (100%) 3 minutes. Stir. Microwave 2 to 3 minutes longer, stirring every minute, until the mixture is very thick and boils. Ask an adult to remove the cup from the microwave.

4. Using potholders to hold the cup in place, stir the mixture well. Let stand uncovered 5 minutes.

5. Break or cut into pieces

> 2 milk chocolate bars (1.55 ounces
> each)

6. Stir the chocolate pieces into the pudding. Pour into the serving dishes right away.

7. Cover and refrigerate at least 1 hour or until chilled. Serve with

> Whipped topping or whipped cream.

HINT: *If you stir the pudding once a minute after it's warm, it will mix evenly and won't boil over. When you pour the pudding into the serving dishes right after stirring in the chocolate pieces they won't melt completely, and add a delicious "crunch" to the pudding.*

Yummy Bites (page 138), Triple Chocolate Pudding

Fudgy Peppermint Sauce

1 1/2 cups sauce

INGREDIENTS

Semisweet
  chocolate chips
Peppermint patties
Canned evaporated
  milk

UTENSILS

Microwavable
  4-cup glass
  measuring cup
Can opener
Long-handled
  spoon

1. Put in the glass measuring cup

> 1 package (6 ounces) semisweet
>   chocolate chips (1 cup)
> 6 small peppermint patties (about
>   1 1/4-inch size)
> 1 can (5 1/2 ounces) evaporated
>   milk

2. Microwave uncovered on High
(100%) 1 1/2 minutes. Stir.

3. Microwave 1 to 2 minutes longer or
until mixture can be stirred smooth. Let
stand uncovered about 5 minutes.

4. Serve over ice cream, angel food cake
or brownies if you like.

5. Cover and refrigerate any leftover
sauce. (It will get firm.)

PEANUT BUTTER FUDGE SAUCE: Substitute
1/4 cup peanut butter for the peppermint
patties.

HINT: *For an extra-special treat, dip fresh
fruit chunks, such as bananas, pineapple or strawberries, or cookies or
doughnut holes into sauce.*

*According to
Maria, this
sauce has every-
thing going for it.
She explained,
"It's fun, easy
and really tastes
good." We think
that's the perfect
combination!*

Puffy Pebble Pie

8 servings

INGREDIENTS

Large jet-puffed
  marshmallows or
  miniature
  marshmallows
Milk
Chocolate malted
  milk powder
Whipping (heavy)
  cream
Malted milk candies
  (small or regular)
8-inch chocolate
  cookie crumb crust

UTENSILS

Large (3-quart or
  larger)
  microwavable
  bowl or casserole
Microwavable glass
  measuring cup
Measuring spoons
Electric mixer
Spoon
Rubber scraper

1. Put in the large bowl

> 1 package (10 ounces) large jet-puffed
> marshmallows or 4 cups miniature
> marshmallows

2. Mix in the glass measuring cup until
dissolved, then pour over the marshmallows

> 1/3 cup milk
> 2 tablespoons chocolate malted milk
> powder

3. Microwave uncovered on High
(100%) 2 1/2 to 3 1/2 minutes or until
the mixture can be stirred smooth.

4. Refrigerate about 20 minutes, stirring
2 times, until the mixture mounds slightly
when dropped from a spoon. Mixture
should not be warm. (If mixture becomes
too thick, microwave on High [100%] 10
to 15 seconds.)

5. Beat on high speed with the electric
mixer about 3 minutes or until stiff

> 1 1/2 cups whipping (heavy) cream

6. Fold the whipped cream into the
marshmallow mixture along with

> 1 cup small malted milk candies

7. Pour the mixture into the crust,
mounding it in the middle, then decorate
with

> 1 cup small malted milk candies

8. Cover and freeze at least 2 hours or
until firm. Top with more whipped cream
if you like.

HINT: *Marshmallows will puff up a lot at
first, then go down when they're
stirred.*

Murad *told us,
"It tasted great. It
was the most de-
licious—I love it
a lot!" Thanks for
the compliment,
Murad!*

Strawberry Cake

8 servings

INGREDIENTS	UTENSILS
All-purpose flour	Scissors
Strawberry-flavored gelatin	Waxed paper
Baking soda	Microwavable 8-inch round dish
Salt	Dry measuring cups
Fruit punch	Measuring spoons
Vegetable oil	Medium bowl
Vanilla	Long-handled spoon
Egg	Liquid measuring cup
Frozen whipped topping, thawed	Rubber scraper
Fresh strawberries	Microwavable dinner plate
	Potholders
	Toothpick
	Heatproof serving plate
	Table knife or metal spatula
	Colander
	Paper towels

1. Using scissors, cut a piece of waxed paper to fit the bottom of the round dish. Set aside.

Strawberry Cake

2. Mix together in the medium bowl (you will be able to see small lumps even after stirring)

> 1 1/2 cups all-purpose flour
> 1 package (3 ounces) strawberry-flavored gelatin
> 1 teaspoon baking soda
> 1/2 teaspoon salt

3. Stir into the dry mixture in the bowl until well blended

> 3/4 cup fruit punch
> 1/4 cup vegetable oil
> 1 teaspoon vanilla
> 1 egg

4. Pour the batter into the wax paper-lined round dish. Put the microwavable dinner plate upside down in the microwave. Put the round dish on top of the plate. Microwave uncovered on High (100%) 2 minutes. Turn the dish 1/2 turn. Microwave 2 to 4 minutes longer or until a toothpick poked in center comes out clean and the top is almost dry. Using potholders, remove the dish from the microwave.

5. Let the cake stand uncovered on a flat, heatproof surface (not wire rack) 10 minutes.

6. Ask an adult to help put the serving plate upside down over the cake. Hold the plate to the round dish handles and turn both upside down so the cake falls onto the serving plate. Remove the round dish and pull off the waxed paper. Cool the cake completely.

7. Frost the cake with

> 1 container (4 ounces) frozen whipped topping, thawed

8. Refrigerate at least 1 hour or until chilled.

9. Rinse in a colander and gently dry with paper towels

> Fresh strawberries

10. Remove the strawberry stems if you like. Decorate the cake with the strawberries just before serving. Refrigerate any remaining cake.

RASPBERRY CAKE: Use raspberry-flavored gelatin and fresh raspberries in place of the strawberry-flavored gelatin and the fresh strawberries.

HINT: *This cake will be the same color as the gelatin you use.*

Alisha was very adventurous when she made this cake. She said, "I would make this again . . . I had never made a cake before." We bet Alisha will start baking lots of cakes from now on.

Ruffled Cupcakes

18 cupcakes

INGREDIENTS
Great Chocolate Cake batter (page 133)

UTENSILS
Same as for Great Chocolate Cake Microwavable 6-cup muffin ring Wax-coated candy papers or paper baking cups

1. Ask an adult to help. Use 4 × 5-inch wax-coated candy papers or paper baking cups, available at household paper or specialty baking equipment stores.

2. Put 2 pieces of paper crosswise on top of each muffin cup. Use a small glass and push straight down against the sides so the edges of the papers ruffle but the paper in the cup lies flat.

3. Mix the batter as directed in Great Chocolate Cake through step 2.

4. Fill each of the 6 cups with about 2 tablespoons batter and microwave uncovered on high (100%) 1 minute. Turn the ring 1/4 turn. Microwave 1 1/2 to 1 3/4 minutes longer, turning ring 1/4 turn every minute. Immediately sprinkle 1 teaspoon chips over each cupcake. Repeat 2 more times.

Great Chocolate Cake

8 servings

INGREDIENTS

All-purpose flour
Packed brown
  sugar
Cocoa
Baking soda
Salt
Water
Vegetable oil
Vinegar
Vanilla
Candy-coated
  chocolate chips

UTENSILS

Large bowl
Long-handled
  spoon
Dry measuring cups
Metal spatula or
  straight-edged
  knife
Liquid measuring
  cup
Measuring spoons
Rubber scraper
Microwavable
  8-inch round dish
Microwavable
  9-inch glass pie
  plate
Potholders
Toothpick

1. Mix together in the large bowl until well blended

> 1 2/3 cups all-purpose flour
> 1 cup packed brown sugar
> 1/4 cup cocoa
> 1 teaspoon baking soda
> 1/2 teaspoon salt

2. Mix into the dry mixture in the bowl until well blended

> 1 cup water
> 1/3 cup vegetable oil
> 1 teaspoon vinegar
> 1/2 teaspoon vanilla

3. Pour into the round dish. Put the glass pie plate upside down in the microwave. Put the round dish on top of the pie plate. Microwave uncovered on Medium (50%) 5 minutes. Turn the dish 1/4 turn.

4. Microwave on Medium (50%) 10 to 14 minutes longer, turning the dish 1/4 turn every 5 minutes, until a toothpick poked in the center comes out clean. Using potholders, remove the dish from the microwave.

5. Immediately sprinkle evenly over the cake

> 1/2 cup candy-coated chocolate chips

6. Let stand uncovered on a flat, heat-proof surface (not wire rack) 10 minutes. Serve this cake right from the dish.

HINT: *Be sure to use baking cocoa and not a cocoa mix made for beverages. For variety, try other flavors of chips such as peanut butter, milk chocolate or white chocolate.*

Pineapple Puddle Cakes

4 servings

INGREDIENTS

Packed brown
  sugar
Margarine or butter
Light corn syrup
Canned sliced
  pineapple
Maraschino
  cherries
Bisquick baking mix
Granulated sugar
Egg

UTENSILS

Microwavable glass
  measuring cup
Dry measuring cups
Table knife
Measuring spoons
Potholders
4 microwavable
  10-ounce custard
  cups
Can opener
Strainer
Liquid measuring
  cup
Bowl to catch
  pineapple juice
Medium bowl
Large spoon
Toothpick
Fork
4 dessert plates

1. Put in the glass measuring cup

> 1/2 cup packed brown sugar
> 1/4 cup margarine or butter
> 2 tablespoons light corn syrup

2. Microwave uncovered on High (100%) 45 to 60 seconds or until melted and bubbly. Stir.

3. Carefully divide the sugar mixture evenly among the 4 custard cups (about 2 tablespoons in each cup).

4. Put the strainer over a bowl in the sink and pour in to drain, saving the juice,

> 1 can (8 ounces) sliced pineapple

5. Put 1 slice of pineapple in each custard cup. Put the strainer in the sink and put 4 cherries in the strainer to drain. Put in the center of *each* pineapple slice

> 1 maraschino cherry

6. Measure out 1/3 cup of the pineapple juice. (If there is not quite enough, add a little water.) Pour the juice into the medium bowl.

7. Stir in and beat hard by hand for 30 seconds

> 1 cup Bisquick baking mix
> 1/4 cup granulated sugar
> 1 egg

8. Pour the same amount of batter (about 1/3 cup) into each custard cup over the top of fruit.

9. Put the custard cups in a circle about 1 inch apart in the microwave. Microwave uncovered on High (100%) 3 minutes.

10. Ask an adult to use potholders and turn each custard cup 1/2 turn. Microwave 2 or 3 minutes longer or until a toothpick poked in the centers of the cakes comes out clean.

11. Ask an adult to remove the custard cups from the microwave. Let the cups stand uncovered on a flat, heatproof surface (not a wire rack) 5 minutes.

12. Holding each cup with a potholder, carefully pull edge of cake away from cup with a fork. Turn each cake over onto a dessert plate. Caramel mixture will run down side of cake and form a puddle. You may need to spoon out a little of the caramel mixture that sticks to the cups. Wait about 15 minutes before eating the cake—the pineapple will be very hot at first!

Carrie told us, "It can get messy while you're making it, and I like making messes! I invite my friends over to eat the cakes with me." Well, Carrie, have fun and don't forget to clean up your mess when you're done.

WINTER WONDERS

These recipes will warm up any cold day. Serve Hot Cocoa and Pineapple Puddle Cakes for the perfect after-skating snack.

My Hot Cocoa (page 39)
Brown-sugared Apples (page 76)
Turkey Lurkey Chili (page 107)
Chunky Chowder (page 112)
Chiliburger Pie (page 94)
Awesome Apple Crisp (page 124)
Pineapple Puddle Cakes (left)

Soft Pumpkin Faces

8 cookies

INGREDIENTS

All-purpose flour
Packed dark brown
 sugar
Canned pumpkin
Ground cinnamon
Baking powder
Salt
Vegetable oil
Vanilla
Egg
Different kinds of
 candies and nuts
 (candy corn,
 ring-shaped hard
 candies, peanuts,
 cashews, etc.)

UTENSILS

Microwavable
 paper towels
Microwavable
 dinner plate
Medium bowl
Dry measuring cups
Measuring spoons
Long-handled
 spoon
Rubber scraper
Wire cooling rack

1. Put 1 paper towel on the dinner plate. Set aside.

2. Mix together with the spoon in the medium bowl

> 1 cup all-purpose flour
> 1/2 cup packed dark brown sugar
> 1/2 cup canned pumpkin
> 1 teaspoon ground cinnamon
> 1/2 teaspoon baking powder
> 1/4 teaspoon salt
> 2 tablespoons vegetable oil
> 1 teaspoon vanilla
> 1 egg

3. Make 3 cookies at a time. Drop the dough by 1/4 cupfuls in a circle on the paper towel-lined plate.

4. Flatten the dough a little and smooth it to make a 3-inch circle. Decorate to make fun faces and designs, pushing into dough a little, with

> Different kinds of candies and nuts (candy corn, ring-shaped hard candies, peanuts, cashews, etc.)

5. Microwave uncovered on High (100%) 1 minute. Turn the plate 1/2 turn. Microwave uncovered 1 to 2 minutes longer, checking every 30 seconds, until the cookies are puffed and dry. Slide cookies, still on the paper towel, onto the cooling rack. Cool 5 minutes. Carefully take the cookies off the paper towel and put them on the cooling rack.

6. Repeat with remaining paper towel and cookie dough.

HINT: *Microwaving the soft cookies on a paper towel helps keep the bottoms dry, and cooling on a rack helps keep them dry as well.*

Spider Webs (page 150), Peanut-Popcorn Balls (page 145), Soft Pumpkin Faces

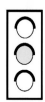

Yummy Bites

12 servings

INGREDIENTS	UTENSILS
Margarine or butter	12 paper baking
Semisweet	cups
chocolate chips	Microwavable
Sugar	muffin ring
All-purpose flour	Microwavable
Vanilla	4-cup glass
Egg	measuring cup
Bite-size	Table knife or metal
chocolate-covered	spatula
peanut butter cup	Dry measuring cups
candies	Long-handled
	spoon
	Measuring spoons
	Tablespoon
	Rubber scraper
	Potholders
	Wire cooling rack

1. Put 6 of the paper baking cups in the microwavable muffin ring. Spread the other 6 out on the counter.

2. Put in the glass measuring cup

> 1/4 cup margarine or butter
> 1/2 cup semisweet chocolate chips

3. Microwave uncovered on High (100%) 1 to 1 1/2 minutes or until the mixture can be stirred smooth. Cool a few minutes.

4. Mix into the chocolate until smooth (batter will be stiff)

> 1/2 cup sugar
> 1/2 cup all-purpose flour
> 1 teaspoon vanilla
> 1 egg

5. Divide the batter evenly among all 12 baking cups (about 1 rounded tablespoon each). Put into the center of the batter in *each* cup, pressing down a little,

> 1 bite-size chocolate-covered peanut butter cup candy

6. Microwave the 6 filled cups in the ring uncovered on High (100%) 1 minute. Turn the ring 1/2 turn. Microwave 30 seconds to 1 1/2 minutes longer, checking every 30 seconds, until the batter looks dry on top. Using potholders, remove the ring from the microwave.

7. Let stand uncovered 2 minutes. Move the cooked bites to the cooling rack. Put the other 6 filled baking cups in the muffin ring. Microwave the same way.

8. Cool at least 15 minutes before eating.

HINT: *Chocolate chips don't change their shape when melted in the microwave. If they're shiny, they can be stirred smooth. Because there is lots of sugar in this recipe, it is very important to turn the ring so the bites cook evenly.*

Melissa is a thoughtful hostess. She wants to share one of her favorite recipes with her friends. She told us, "Tastes so-o-o good! It's so easy and you get to put in peanut butter cups. I can make it for my friends for a real treat."

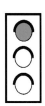

Gooey Marshmallow Bars

18 bars

INGREDIENTS	UTENSILS
Peanut butter	Table knife or metal
Graham cracker	spatula
squares	Microwavable
Miniature	8-inch square dish
marshmallows	Dry measuring cups
Chopped salted	Cutting board
peanuts	Sharp knife

1. Spread peanut butter on 1 side of

> 18 graham cracker squares (2 1/2 inches each)

2. Fit 9 of the graham crackers, peanut butter side up, to cover the bottom of the square dish. Sprinkle evenly over the top

> 1 1/2 cups miniature marshmallows

3. Sprinkle over the marshmallows

> 1/2 cup chopped salted peanuts

4. Put the rest of the graham crackers, peanut butter sides down, on top of the peanuts.

5. Microwave uncovered on High (100%) 1 to 2 minutes or until the marshmallows are soft and squishy.

6. Cool at least 15 minutes. Cut between the crackers to make squares. Cut each square in half.

HINT: *A table knife rubbed with a little vegetable oil will make it easier to cut through these gooey bars. If you like, a few chocolate chips can be sprinkled over the marshmallows before you put the top graham crackers on.*

Banana Cookie Bars

16 bars

INGREDIENTS

Shortbread cookies
Vanilla
  ready-to-spread
  frosting
Banana
Bisquick baking mix
Egg
Chopped salted
  peanuts

UTENSILS

Microwavable
  8-inch square dish
Dry measuring cups
Rubber scraper
Table knife or metal
  spatula
Fork
Medium bowl
Large spoon
Waxed paper
Potholders
Toothpick
Cutting board
Sharp knife
Wire cooling rack

1. Arrange to fit the bottom of the square dish

> 16 shortbread cookies (each about 1 1/2 inches square)

2. Measure out 1 cup of frosting from

> vanilla ready-to-spread frosting

3. Put 1/2 cup of the frosting in the medium bowl. Save the remaining 1/2 cup to frost the top.

4. Break into pieces and add to the frosting in the bowl, mashing with a fork until smooth,

> 1 medium banana

5. Stir in until well blended

> 3/4 cup Bisquick baking mix
> 1 egg

6. Pour the batter over the cookies, spreading evenly.

7. Cover with waxed paper, curled side down. Microwave on High (100%) 2 minutes. Turn the dish 1/2 turn. Microwave 2 to 3 minutes longer or until a toothpick poked in the center comes out clean. Carefully lift the edge of waxed paper farthest away from you, to let the steam out, then remove the waxed paper.

8. Using potholders, remove the dish from the microwave. Cool the bars completely on the cooling rack.

9. Frost with the frosting you saved. Sprinkle with

> 1/4 cup chopped salted peanuts

10. Cut into 16 squares.

Pecan-Marshmallow Drops

20 candies

INGREDIENTS	UTENSILS
Miniature marshmallows	Waxed paper
Semisweet chocolate chips	Cookie sheet
Milk	Medium micro-wavable bowl
Pecan halves	Dry measuring cups
Vanilla	Table knife or metal spatula
	Measuring spoons
	Long-handled spoon

1. Put waxed paper, curled side down, over the cookie sheet.

2. Put in the medium bowl

> 1 cup miniature marshmallows
> 1/2 cup semisweet chocolate chips
> 1 tablespoon milk

3. Cover with waxed paper. Microwave on High (100%) 1 to 2 minutes, stirring every minute, until the marshmallows are melted and the mixture is smooth.

4. Stir in until well blended

> 1 cup pecan halves
> 1/4 teaspoon vanilla

5. Drop the mixture, with 3 pecan halves per cluster, onto cookie sheet. Let stand uncovered about 30 minutes or until firm.

PEANUTTY MARSHMALLOW DROPS: Use peanuts in place of pecans, and peanut butter chips in place of chocolate chips.

Mike *has big plans for these drops. He said, "They're very good for a party."*

Chocolate S'more Squares

18 candies

INGREDIENTS

Butter or margarine
Milk chocolate
 chips
Light corn syrup
Margarine or butter
Vanilla
Ground cinnamon
Honey graham
 cereal
Miniature
 marshmallows

UTENSILS

9-inch square pan
Microwavable
 3-quart casserole
 with lid
Dry measuring cups
Liquid measuring
 cup
Measuring spoons
Potholders
Long-handled
 spoon
Large spoon

1. Butter the pan. Set aside.

2. Mix in the 3-quart casserole

> 31 cup milk chocolate chips
> 1/3 cup light corn syrup
> 1 tablespoon margarine or butter
> 1/2 teaspoon vanilla
> 1/4 teaspoon ground cinnamon

3. Cover with the lid and microwave on High (100%) 2 to 3 minutes or until boiling. Carefully remove the lid, lifting from the side away from you, to let the steam out. Stir.

4. Fold in until completely coated with chocolate

> 4 cups honey graham cereal

5. Fold in

> 1 1/2 cups miniature marshmallows

6. Coat the back of a large spoon with butter and use it to press the cereal mixture evenly in the buttered pan. Let stand about 1 hour or until cool. Cut into about 2-inch squares.

Chocolate S'more Squares (top), Pecan-Marshmallow Drops (page 141) (bottom)

Double Whammy Fudge

About 5 dozen candies

INGREDIENTS

Canned sweetened
  condensed milk
Semisweet
  chocolate chips
Unsweetened
  chocolate
Vanilla
Chopped nuts

UTENSILS

8-inch square pan
Waxed paper
Microwavable
  medium bowl
Can opener
Long-handled
  spoon
Potholders
Measuring spoons
Dry measuring cups
Cutting board
Sharp knife

1. Line the bottom and sides of the pan with waxed paper, leaving 1 inch of waxed paper over sides of pan. Tear off 2 pieces of waxed paper about 15 inches long. Fold each of the long sides 2 inches toward the center. Lay 1 piece evenly across the pan and push it down into the corners. Lay the other piece across the pan the other way and crease the bottom corners.

Line the bottom and sides of the pan with waxed paper. Lift the candy out of the pan using the waxed paper "handles."

2. Put in the medium bowl

> 1 can (14 ounces) sweetened condensed milk
> 1 package (12 ounces) semisweet chocolate chips (2 cups)
> 1 ounce unsweetened chocolate

3. Microwave uncovered on High (100%) 1 to 3 minutes, stirring after 1 minute, until the chocolate is melted and the mixture can be stirred smooth.

4. Stir in

> 1 teaspoon vanilla
> 1 1/2 cups chopped nuts

5. Spread evenly in the pan. Refrigerate about 2 hours or until firm.

6. Lift the candy out of the pan using the waxed paper "handles." Cut into 1-inch squares.

Peanut-Popcorn Balls

4 popcorn balls

INGREDIENTS	UTENSILS
Packed brown sugar	Large microwavable bowl
Corn syrup	Dry measuring cups
Creamy peanut butter	Measuring spoons
Dash of salt	Potholders
Popped popcorn	Long-handled spoon
Salted peanuts	Waxed paper
	Plastic wrap

1. Mix together in the large bowl

> 1/4 cup packed brown sugar
> 1/4 cup corn syrup
> 2 tablespoons creamy peanut butter
> Dash of salt

2. Microwave uncovered on High (100%) 1 to 1 1/2 or until the mixture begins to bubble. Stir.

3. Stir in until well coated

> 4 cups popped popcorn (about 1/4 cup unpopped)
> 1/2 cup salted peanuts

4. Let stand uncovered 5 minutes or until cool enough to touch.

5. Dip your hands in cold water, then firmly press the popcorn mixture to make 4 balls about the size of tennis balls. Place the balls on waxed paper. Let stand about 30 minutes or until completely cool. Wrap in waxed paper or plastic wrap.

HALLOWEEN HITS

Plan a Halloween party with all kinds of spooky, scary and delicious recipes. You'll probably have just as much fun making the food as eating it!

Chilly Day Cinnamon Cider (page 39)
Caramel Apples (page 38)
Peanut-Popcorn Balls (left)
Soft Pumpkin Faces (page 136)
Spider Webs (page 150)

Following pages: Launching Rocket Cones (page 148), Finger Dough (page 151), Puffy Pebble Pie (page 129)

Launching Rocket Cones

4 rockets

INGREDIENTS

Cone-shaped sugar cones

Marshmallows

Plain or chocolate-covered graham cracker squares*

Vanilla or chocolate ready-to-spread frosting

Candy and nuts for decoration (string licorice, colored sprinkles, etc.)

UTENSILS

Four 4- or 5-ounce paper drinking cups

Scissors

Spoon

Cookie sheet

Waxed paper

Microwavable 2-cup glass measuring cup

Rubber scraper

Dry measuring cups

Cutting board

Sharp serrated knife

1. Make your own rocket "launchers" by cutting an "X" in the bottoms of the paper cups. Carefully poke the pointed end of each cone into the "X." Be sure it's standing straight using

4 cone-shaped sugar cones

* You will only need 8 chocolate-covered crackers for 16 fins, but you should have extra on hand just in case some break while cutting.

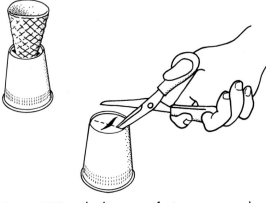

Cut an "X" in the bottoms of paper cups and carefully poke the pointed end of the cone into the "X."

2. Cut one of the marshmallows into fourths. Drop one piece into each cone. Push into each cone on top of the little piece.

4 large marshmallows

3. Put the cups with cones in a circle in the microwave. Microwave uncovered on High (100%) 15 to 30 seconds or until the marshmallows puff way up. Carefully remove the cups from the microwave. (Marshmallows will go down into the cone as they cool.) If the marshmallows puff out of the cones, use a small spoon and carefully push them back in.

4. Cool completely. Save the "launchers" to use again.

5. Cut into 4 pieces, using a "sawing" motion (see diagram)

4 plain or chocolate-covered graham cracker squares (about 2 1/2 inches)

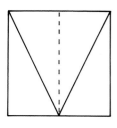

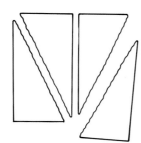

Cut each graham cracker into 4 triangles as shown.

6. Put the waxed paper on the cookie sheet. Arrange on the waxed paper so they are spread out

> 4 graham cracker squares (about 2 1/2 inches)

7. Put in the glass measuring cup

> 1 cup vanilla or chocolate ready-to-spread frosting

8. Microwave on High (100%) 15 to 30 seconds or until almost melted. Stir until smooth.

9. With 1 hand, tip the measuring cup. With your other hand, carefully roll each cone in the frosting to cover the outside. Put the open end of the cone down on graham cracker square. A little frosting should drip down onto the graham cracker to glue it on.

10. Put the graham cracker triangles on the base of the cones to make rocket "fins."

11. Let dry at least 1 hour. Reheat frosting 10 to 15 seconds if necessary and decorate the rockets as you like with

> Candy and nuts for decoration (string licorice, colored sprinkles, etc.)

HINTS: *Not only do you get to make rockets, but the rocket "launcher," too! Cones with even tops work best if you want the rocket to aim straight up.*

An easy way to cut marshmallows is first to dip the scissors in water—then the marshmallows won't stick to the blades.

*Maybe **Rachel** will be an astronaut one day— she thinks that Launching Rocket Cones are out of this world. Her comment is, "It tastes good and is easy to prepare, plus it looks good . . . it really looked like a rocket!"*

Spider Webs

6 webs

INGREDIENTS

Pretzel sticks
Vanilla-flavored
  candy coating*

UTENSILS

Waxed paper
2 cookie sheets
Cutting board
Sharp knife
Microwavable
  2-cup glass
  measuring cup
Spoon

1. Put waxed paper curled side down over each of the cookie sheets.

2. Arrange in 6 groups of 8 on the waxed paper to look like spokes of a wheel

48 pretzel sticks

3. Cut each block in half and put in the glass measuring cup

4 ounces (4 blocks) vanilla-flavored candy coating

4. Microwave uncovered on High (100%) 2 minutes. Stir until smooth. If all the lumps cannot be stirred out, microwave 30 seconds longer.

5. Spoon or pour a small amount candy coating in the middle of each group of pretzels to hold it together. Spoon a thin stream of melted candy coating in 2 circles (small and large) to form the strands of the web.

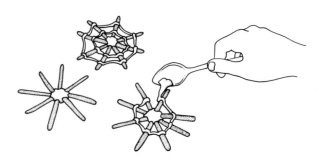

6. Refrigerate about 15 minutes or until firm.

7. Carefully remove from waxed paper.

HINTS: *Arrange 3 groups of pretzels on each cookie sheet far enough apart so the pretzels do not touch each other. You may want some help with this recipe.*

To make a spider, cut 3 tiny snips with kitchen scissors close to each other on opposite sides of a raisin. Spread apart to look like spider legs. Press into the candy coating before it hardens.

* Vanilla-flavored candy coating is purchased in 1-pound packages divided into blocks. There's enough left over to make Spider Webs again.

Finger Dough

About 1/2 pound

INGREDIENTS

Bisquick baking mix
Salt
Cream of tartar
Water
Food color

UTENSILS

Dry measuring cups
Measuring spoons
Microwavable
 4-cup glass
 measuring cup
Liquid measuring
 cup
Spoon
Rubber scraper
Tightly covered
 container or
 plastic bag

1. Mix together in the glass measuring cup

> 1 1/4 cups Bisquick baking mix
> 1/4 cup salt
> 1 teaspoon cream of tartar

2. Mix in the liquid measuring cup

> 1 cup water
> 1 teaspoon food color

3. Stir the liquid into the dry mixture, a little at a time, until all the liquid is added. Microwave uncovered on High (100%) 1 minute.

4. Scrape the mixture from the side of the cup and stir.

5. Microwave uncovered on High (100%) 2 to 3 minutes longer, stirring every minute, until the mixture forms sort of a ball.

6. Let the dough stand uncovered about 3 minutes.

7. Spoon out of the measuring cup. Knead in your hands or on the counter about 1 minute or until smooth. (If the dough is sticky, add 1 to 2 tablespoons of Bisquick.) Cool about 15 minutes.

8. Use to make your favorite shapes and designs. Store in a tightly covered container.

HINTS: *This bold-colored dough is fun to play with but not usually eaten. For pastel-colored dough, use less food color. To knead means to curve your fingers and fold the dough toward you, then push it away with the heels of your hands, using a quick rocking motion.*

METRIC CONVERSION GUIDE

U.S. UNITS	CANADIAN METRIC	AUSTRALIAN METRIC
Volume		
1/4 teaspoon	1 mL	1 ml
1/2 teaspoon	2 mL	2 ml
1 teaspoon	5 mL	5 ml
1 tablespoon	15 mL	20 ml
1/4 cup	50 mL	60 ml
1/3 cup	75 mL	80 ml
1/2 cup	125 mL	125 ml
2/3 cup	150 mL	170 ml
3/4 cup	175 mL	190 ml
1 cup	250 mL	250 ml
1 quart	1 liter	1 liter
1 1/2 quarts	1.5 liter	1.5 liter
2 quarts	2 liters	2 liters
2 1/2 quarts	2.5 liters	2.5 liters
3 quarts	3 liters	3 liters
4 quarts	4 liters	4 liters
Weight		
1 ounce	30 grams	30 grams
2 ounces	55 grams	60 grams
3 ounces	85 grams	90 grams
4 ounces (1/4 pound)	115 grams	125 grams
8 ounces (1/2 pound)	225 grams	225 grams
16 ounces (1 pound)	455 grams	500 grams
1 pound	455 grams	1/2 kilogram

Measurements		**Temperatures**	
Inches	Centimeters	Fahrenheit	Celsius
1	2.5	32°	0°
2	5.0	212°	100°
3	7.5	250°	120°
4	10.0	275°	140°
5	12.5	300°	150°
6	15.0	325°	160°
7	17.5	350°	180°
8	20.5	375°	190°
9	23.0	400°	200°
10	25.5	425°	220°
11	28.0	450°	230°
12	30.5	475°	240°
13	33.0	500°	260°
14	35.5		
15	38.0		

NOTE

The recipes in this cookbook have not been developed or tested using metric measures. When converting recipes to metric, some variations in quality may be noted.

INDEX